Praise for Susan Bacon's
The History Teacher

". . . scrupulously researched, cagily and compellingly plotted and eminently credible . . . a pleasure to read, written, sentence by sentence, with the eye of a shrewd observer and the ear of a writer who knows language is music."

— BRUCE WEBER,
JOURNALIST AND AUTHOR

" . . . fresh and eye-opening . . . a lively, classic page-turner"

— EMILY YELLIN,
JOURNALIST AND AUTHOR

" . . . a riveting suspense thriller of a novel by an author with an impressively reader-engaging narrative storytelling style . . ."

— MIDWEST BOOK REVIEW

Praise for Susan Bacon's
The Art Collector

". . . an intriguing mystery story that draws you in and keeps you guessing but also a vibrant portrayal of the downtown art scene in Manhattan in the '70s and '80s, and the Deep South back in the '60s . . ."

— EBET ROBERTS,
LEGENDARY PHOTOGRAPHER OF
MANHATTAN'S MUSIC SCENE

". . . the mystery is compelling and takes unexpected turns, and it's supported by a steady pace and unique characters. . . An intriguing whodunit with memorable characters."

— KIRKUS REVIEWS

". . . a compelling page-turner . . . The Memphis chapters are alive with the sounds and smells of the region."

— JESSE DAVIS, MEMPHIS MAGAZINE

ALSO BY SUSAN BACON

The History Teacher
The Art Collector

Alice *Adrift*

A NOVEL

SUSAN BACON

Porter Street Press

In Chapter 12, material quoted from a review of Gustav Flaubert's letters is from a book review by Jesse Kornbluth of *The Letters of Gustave-Flaubert*, edited by Francis Steegmuller. The review, published on March 27, 2018, appeared on the HeadButler.com website @ https://headbutler.com/reviews/letters-gustave-flaubert/.

Alice Adrift is a work of fiction. All dialogue and specific events, and all characters except for certain well-known historic and/or popular figures, are products of the author's imagination and are not to be interpreted or construed as real. Where actual historical and popular figures do appear, the situations, incidents and dialogue concerning those figures are fictional and *not* intended to depict actual events or to suggest that this work is anything other than fiction. In all other respects, any resemblance to actual persons, living or dead, events, or locations is entirely coincidental.

Interior book design by Robert Harrison

Book cover design by www.ebooklaunch.com

Portrait by Fran Doggrell

Library of Congress Cataloging-in-Publication Data has been applied for.

Library of Congress Control Number: 2025901285

ISBN: 978-1-7330827-5-4

ISBN (ebook): 978-1-7330827-7-8

Porter Street Press

PART I

Beware the Jabberwock, my son!
The jaws that bite, the claws that catch!
Beware the Jubjub bird, and shun
The furious Bandersnatch!

—*Jabberwocky*, Lewis Carroll

CHAPTER 1

Alice & David
May 1997

Alice was waiting for an epiphany. His, not hers. She assumed a time would come when he would ask himself "What on earth have I done?" But she couldn't imagine, back then when he was still living in what is now her home, how long it would take. At first, she thought about it in terms of weeks. Then months. Then, finally, as each day passed without a trace of any remorse or grief or guilt or shame, she knew it would be years. And that it was quite possible that by the time he came to know all that she knew, it would be of no value—like a punishment exacted so long after the crime that its value is lost to the victim.

Once he came close, not long after she had first confronted him about the affair and he had stared at her aghast as if it were she, not he, who was crazy. A child had died, the son of someone they barely knew. This little boy had walked into the Chesapeake Bay during a family weekend, walked away from a house filled with aunts and uncles and cousins and a mother and father who were drinking beer and basking in the simple safety of an extended family. The child went off alone for a swim and never came back. They called the rescue squad and the neighbors and launched a two-day search, finally dredging the bay and finding the lost boy.

It was such a painful story that David took it on as part of him and made it his own. Driving to the funeral, somewhere out in Northern Virginia, he wept and begged her forgiveness, as if there were some connection between what he had done and this poor family's grief.

"It's my fault. It's all my fault," he said over and over, looking pale and sleepless, his skin drawn tighter, it seemed, around his face. "What can I do to make it right?" His voice had that taut quality, gravelly and tense.

Even then, his pain exposed, the apology seemed disingenuous.

"I don't know," she said. Sometimes it seemed as if he were missing a part of him, a barometer that could tell the difference between the truth and whatever words he spoke.

They drove past a string of newly built homes, big ones made of shiny red bricks and fieldstones on naked lots. She could picture their insides—cool, marbled foyers with double-height ceilings and massive contemporary chandeliers hanging like pendulums in ridiculously splendid center halls. They had been to a house like that once, to a Christmas party. That was back in the early nineties before all their friends started moving to big old houses and buying big-screen TVs. Alice and David lived in a bungalow, one they had bought in the mid-eighties for next to nothing and turned inside out until it fit them precisely. He was an architect.

Sitting there in the front seat, watching David gather himself up for the child's funeral, she remembered the party itself as having a sterile quality to it. The decorator had just finished the place, and everything matched. There was no clutter—no thumbed-through magazines, no unsharpened pencils, no un-opened mail lying about. The host was a client of David's who made more money in a year than they had made in their lifetime together. David hadn't designed the house, just the interior of the pool house.

He had been uncomfortable at the party. His client and the guests had too much money and too much power. He had tried to be witty, almost jovial, which was not his way. David could be stunning—lean and intense, with his deep brown eyes and chis-eled face. But on this night, his suit cut a bit too loose, his hair a tad too long, he didn't fit in smoothly. When they arrived, Alice overheard the host telling David, "Your wife is just lovely," sounding almost surprised. Alice hadn't known anyone and stood listening silently to all the jibber-jabber about what private school which child would attend and how some soccer coach behaved badly at the game that had taken place so many weeks before that it should have been lost to the collective memory. She remembered the food was good. Some kind of creamed crabmeat in an elaborate chafing dish, and tenderloin with little rolls and vegetables on skewers. All catered and set out in silver chafing dishes on crisp, white linen cloths.

The funeral was for the child of a contractor David worked with. Neither of them had ever even met the little boy. Alice didn't want to go. She knew it would stir memories of Jeremiah's funeral, triggering emotions she didn't want to feel, that she imagined she was finally moving past. But she didn't tell David.

Later that day, when they carried in the miniature coffin down the center of the vast, suburban church, followed by a train of Catholic families, all heads bowed, they had cried, the two of them, along with everyone else in the church, in a collective heave, chests throbbing, lips quivering. The loss of that child was a measure of all losses, tumbled together and crammed into a moment.

She put on her sunglasses before they left the church. He followed, his eyes red and swollen, and hugged everyone and then they made a beeline for the car. She took off her heels and rubbed her feet, and he turned on the air-conditioning. "Oh, God, Alice." He paused before he started the car, looking drawn and terrified. "Oh, God. What have I done?"

They'd only gotten a few blocks, just clear of the funeral procession, when he pulled the car over to the side of the road. "I can't do it," he said. "I just can't." She waited, knowing that could have meant anything. Then he opened the door and pulled off his seat belt. "You're going to have to drive. I just can't." But, even then, he didn't look her in the eye.

CHAPTER 2

Alice & Tobias
1996

Innocence is not always about what you see or how much you know or the depth of your experience. It is something that some people carry with them from childhood no matter what happens. Perhaps it is about not wanting to know or, maybe not wanting to accept the harm that some people can do to others. In that respect, Alice was somehow innocent. So when it began, when David began his drift in the years that followed Jeremiah's death, she trusted that he would be back, that it was like a stage a child might pass through. Lost, searching for themselves in new places, stepping away so they can somehow blossom separately. And that was as it should have been: the moving away, the coming back. Like the time Tobias, around the age of eight or nine, began spending hour upon hour in his attic room. She would stay away, let him pull back from her a little and have whatever time he needed. Sometimes she would find the detritus of these late evenings of solitude in a corner of his room while she was straightening up. Scrambled jottings, notes from some song he'd been fooling with, a broken guitar string. She learned to leave him be for a while.

Sometimes, he would emerge mid-session and they would connect. "Mom," he said once, coming into her kitchen on a fall evening. "Do you think anybody ever really knows anybody else?" He was earnest and direct. Alice turned away from the sink and dried her hands with deliberateness, giving herself time to think.

"That's a good question," she said. "Yes, as much as they can. I think, for example, a mother knows her children. I think I know you." She realized at once that she had given the wrong answer. He pictured himself, at that moment in his life, as remote and complex. The timing was off. After all, Tobias didn't really know himself yet. That's what he was looking for.

"And what is it you think you know about me?" he asked defensively. Tobias had a rather pronounced nervous tic—not serious enough to be diagnosed as Tourette syndrome. It was his left eye mostly. A blinking that jerked his head slightly to the left. He'd had it for a few years now, and no one had figured out how to get rid of it or what exactly it was, so they all just learned to live with it.

He did it now, that crisp, jerky motion. Left twice. Then it stopped.

She was thinking, I know that you love helpless little furry creatures; that you're an intensely loyal friend. I know you wet your bed when you went to summer camp last year because you missed your home; that you have a poetic bent and you are level-headed but can be anxious in new situations. I know that, even with all your empathy, you used to tease your little brother mercilessly. But she said: "I know you're changing. You're getting older and you're more aware of yourself in relation to the rest of the world. Toby, I think it might be a bit confusing to you."

Then she reached over and stroked his hair away from his eyes—and he ticked left twice. "Stop," he said sharply. And she said, "Why do you ask?"

Then it came, as if from out of nowhere. "Do you think you and Dad would ever get divorced?" It was as if he'd knocked the wind out of her.

"No. I don't."

"Theresa's parents are getting divorced."

"Oh, God, Tobias, is she okay?"

"Yeah, but she says her mother told her you can never really know anybody else."

"That's a curious thing to say."

Tobias looked at her intently, his head still. "She says they've been married like twenty years or something and he's been leading this double life." He kept his gaze on her, as if gauging her reaction. She was sitting now opposite him at the kitchen table. "That's weird, don't you think? I mean, like, what is that? A double life," he said.

"I don't know," she said. She shook her head. "It sounds like he was seeing somebody else, like there was another woman."

"Sounds like he had a fucking other family."

She was startled, not by the language itself but the ease with which he said it. "I don't like the casual way that slipped out."

"Sorry, Mom." He spoke very slowly, with a formal intonation. "I meant to say it sounds to me like Theresa's father, Mr. Mathias, may well have had another fucking family."

They both laughed then. And he twitched a little to the left, pleased with himself.

"Well?" he prodded.

She was peeling an orange, pulling the rippled skin from the fruit. She looked down, watching her own hands in seamless motion.

"Well, what?"

"Well, what about you and Dad?"

"Toby," she said, smiling. "Your father is not leading a double life, I'm sure of that. And we love each other. Love can carry you through just about anything." What a ridiculous cliché, she thought. She believed it, but she wished immediately that she hadn't said it.

That was a few months before everything began to unravel. Later, she would remember that conversation and look back with a combination of sadness and wonder. How could she have been so sure? Maybe it was just that she was sure of her own feelings and what they meant and the tenacity with which she would try to hold on to her marriage.

Later, she would wonder if maybe Theresa's mother was the wiser. But, back then, she'd thought: They're different. They don't love each other or know each other the way we do. No, that's something different—a marriage that just splits apart at the seams, a man with a mistress or some other life. Tobias seemed to take it at face value and grabbed a few slices of orange and took them with him back up to the attic. They didn't speak of it again.

But David was already slipping away. Alice just didn't know. She had never even met Rebecca Adler, never even heard her voice. Of course, she'd seen her at The School, Toby's school, looking frenzied in the halls, searching for one child or another, her crinkly red hair flying about like some tangled nest. She seemed dramatic and overwhelmed. And there was an earthiness about her. She had once brushed up against Alice, dragging her children along, leaving the dank smell of their bodies behind.

Alice could see that she was preposterously beautiful, with that hair, those cheekbones, that lithe body draped in exotic fabrics. She didn't dress like most of the other mothers, frumpy in their dirndl skirts and heavy wooden clogs. She drove a big, old brown truck. The back was always filled with boxes and tools and crates full of tree branches and fabrics and leaves. Alice had seen it in the parking lot nearly every time she came to pick up Tobias. Rebecca helped out at The School. She taught weaving and knitting. She'd organized the planting of the pumpkin patch and made the children's fantastical costumes for the Halloween parade. "She's gifted," everyone at The School agreed.

But Alice didn't know enough to be threatened by her. She lumped her in with most everyone else at The School—odd, well-meaning, a little bit crazy maybe. It wasn't your typical school. Tobias thought they'd sent him there because there was something wrong with him ("They don't even teach reading, Mom," he'd said flatly in the second grade). David was drawn to the place. He liked the idea that they built things, drew them up and built them, just as he did in his everyday life. Alice imagined that, somehow, the place felt safe to him, with its curious combination of rules ("No T-shirts with pictures! And please, no superheroes," said The School Handbook) and anarchy. There was no principal, no administration to speak of. The teachers ran the place. Alice thought they had it backward.

"Fewer rules and a little more structure might be nice," she once told David.

"You're just scared of it," he'd shot back.

"Scared that if there's a problem in the classroom, the only person I can go to is a teacher who speaks guru-speak that I don't understand."

"If you'd just loosen up a bit," he'd said, and then he'd grabbed her and pulled her to him—same as always, as if that would settle it.

"Hands-on. Everything's got to be hands-on with that place," she laughed. "I think that's why you like it so much."

He laughed then. "You know what I want to put my hands on." He smiled and raised his eyebrows up and down like Groucho Marx and slipped his hand under the back of her shirt and unsnapped her bra in a single swift motion.

"What about their poor little stunted brains?" she went on, smacking his hand. Then the conversation ended the same way it always had, with the two of them folding into one another.

CHAPTER 3

Alice & David & Rebecca
October 1996

Alice first met Rebecca Adler a few months later, in late October. Toby's class was going apple picking. It was a Saturday, the first real fall Saturday of the year, the day that sparks memories with its first breath. The sky was cool and crisp and white, the wind of a fresh new season sweeping into place. The leaves had turned reds and yellows and oranges, and the pumpkins were in stock, but no one had any on their doorsteps quite yet. Buoyed by the aura of the day itself, Alice was rummaging through boxes of sweaters and hats that had been stored away since the coming of spring. David had run Tobias over to school and come back flushed and exhilarated. Alice imagined they would use the time alone, that some of that energy was going to flow to her. They didn't get much time alone, not during the day anyway. But David had other ideas. He had to be at work, he said. He was going for coffee, then headed for the office.

By afternoon, she had finished putting away the old summer things and pulling out the woolens. She'd boxed things and bagged them. She'd emptied the cedar closet and sorted coats and sweaters, mittens and hats into various piles. Then she made coffee and sat quietly in the corner of the living room, nursing it, looking out the window at the tall oak in the front yard. Alice had always wanted a house like this when she was young; she'd dreamed it many times—the streets lined with thick oaks and maples, the deep front lawns, the kids running about with bikes and dogs, the quaint front porches. A house full of children. "I'll never live in a neighborhood without sidewalks," she'd told David when they were looking for a house. "If it doesn't have sidewalks, you can't walk around in it. And if you can't walk around in it, it's not really a neighborhood, is it?" He'd liked that. David liked the idea of having a family, the normalcy of it. But Alice actually liked having a family.

Settled in by the window, cradling her coffee, she felt smug for an instant. And then it passed. She knew better. It was always a signal that something was about to go wrong, like a bad omen. Never take anything for granted, her mother had warned her many times. It never failed. Like a few weeks before, when Alice had just made it to the dry cleaner's and she got that great parking spot, right by the front door, and she knew she could run in and out and still make it to school in time to get Toby. She was never late. She never wanted to keep him waiting or to find him inside with a teacher, stranded for a few minutes without his mother. "For God's sake," David would say. "He's nine years old."

But, on that day, when she found a parking place right next to the curb in front of the cleaners, she felt smug. After she'd paid for her clothes, all pressed and bagged up nicely, she couldn't find her car keys. It was a good twenty minutes before the lady who'd grabbed them off the counter realized her mistake and came back with them. So Alice didn't get to school until 3:30 p.m. When she did, Tobias was sitting alone in a corner of the administrative office looking small and lonely and bored. And hadn't she been smug in her happiness, with her neat little family, when they lost Jeremiah. Thinking of it, then, she felt a sadness so intense that she grabbed her stomach. Suddenly, she wanted Tobias back home. And she wondered why David had run off that morning. She realized, in that instant, he wasn't really there anymore. In that moment, the reality of it swept through her like a dark secret and she felt cold and frightened. And just then, Rebecca drove up in front of the house.

She climbed out of the truck with Tobias and her son Adrian, and they ran around to the back of the thing jabbering and laughing. Alice watched as they began to unload the apples, one crate after another, which Adrian and Tobias then proceeded to carry up to the front porch. When Alice opened the door, four full crates of green apples were sitting by the doorstep.

"Surely we can't eat all of these," she said as the three approached, each carrying another crate.

"They're not for you," said Rebecca, in a deep, throaty voice with a thick German accent.

"The pies, Mom," Tobias interjected.

"David said it would be all right," Rebecca said, coming through Alice's front door with a load of the things, slightly out of breath and smiling a dazzling smile that made her look like a young girl.

She said it with a familiarity that took Alice aback. "David?"

"He said we could do the baking here, at his house."

His house. She rolled the words over in her mind. His house. He drove up then and breezed through the front door and, without acknowledging a soul but Rebecca, grabbed her crate and carried it into the kitchen.

"I've been to the store," he said proudly. "Everything's in the car."

Then he and Rebecca both turned without a word to anyone else and went out the front door together. Alice watched them as they walked across the yard. Rebecca was gesticulating with her wiry hands, and he was fixated on her. Alice stood there with her mouth open, watching through the window, seeing something between them that she hadn't seen before and never would have dreamed.

"Mom," Toby said—then again, louder, "Mom. What do we do with the apples?"

She turned away and walked back into the kitchen without answering. Once she got there, she grabbed the tea kettle from the stovetop, looked at the wall and stood very still for an instant. She steadied herself, filled the kettle with water. She set it on the stove, turned on the gas and stopped. Calm down, she said to herself. Just calm down. Her impulse was to scream. To run to the front door and scream at the two of them. But, no, she thought, reaching up to open the cupboard, no. Be cool, she thought. She pulled down a box of tea.

She turned then to see David coming into the kitchen with two huge sacks of groceries. She couldn't remember the last time he'd looked so happy. "Shall we have some tea?" she asked, her voice chilly. He didn't acknowledge her, didn't even look up. When Rebecca came through the kitchen door, still beaming, he told her where to put the other grocery bag, and she rubbed up against him with her elbows as she set it down.

The kitchen was small, and cramming the five of them in there to make pies was, Alice knew, an impossibility. They jockeyed about for a time, unpacking bags of flour and sugars and butter and cream. "We only need to make seven pies," Rebecca said. *Only*, thought Alice. *Dear Jesus, they'll be here all night.* She was struggling with every ounce of her being to maintain her equilibrium while they flirted and fawned and laughed. "Let me see your hands," Rebecca said, beckoning him. When he held them out, she took them in her own and turned them over, examining each one slowly and carefully. "I think we'd better wash them," she said crisply, smiling that schoolgirl smile again. So they went over to the sink, where she soaped his hands for him as he stood just a few feet away from Alice, while Alice stared, unmoving, watching them for what seemed an eternity. It was like a dream to her. She was at once confused and angry and indignant and hurt, standing there with the children and not knowing quite what to do. When she spoke, the words came out bitter and sarcastic: "I think they're clean by now, don't you?"

The children, of course, were oblivious. So too was David. But Rebecca heard Alice and laughed. "Oh," she said sharply, as if startled by the intrusion. "Oh. Yes." She laughed again and turned her head very slowly and looked straight at Alice.

David left the kitchen. Rebecca moved toward Alice, up so close that it frightened her, and when their faces were just a few inches apart, she began to talk. "My husband died for me, you know," she said softly, but her eyes were maniacal in their intensity. "The night before he died, I had a dream. I had a dream that I was dead. I woke up in the middle of the night and told him. We were like two halves, two halves of the same person. Like one soul."

Alice knew the story. She had heard it told many times at The School, of how one Sunday afternoon the men and boys were playing soccer at a school picnic, Rebecca watching with the other mothers and the young children. How Rebecca saw her husband fall, and Adrian, who was maybe five years old at the time, ran over to him crying out "Daddy, Daddy" so loud everyone heard it, and everything stopped. Rebecca sat frozen on a blanket, her daughter Angela nestled in her lap. By the time she got up, there were people all around him. Someone—one of the teachers—was trying mouth-to-mouth resuscitation, pounding on her husband's chest. Then Rebecca ran toward them screaming, "Stop it. Stop it. Stop it now!" Alice imagined her crazy hair flying out behind her as she ran. Then Rebecca fell down next to him, begging, "Dear God, don't take him," first in her normal speaking voice. Then again and again, as it kept getting louder and louder and more hysterical. "Don't take him. Don't take him," she was screaming. One man held her, and another ran off and called the ambulance. All the while, her husband lay there still as a stone.

It had become a kind of legend in their community, at The School—how when the medics finally arrived, Rebecca was calm and still, very nearly catatonic. Then, as they lifted the man onto the stretcher, gently and slowly, a rainbow formed. It stretched from one end of the field to the other and stayed there until the ambulance drove off with Rebecca and Adrian and little Angela and the dead man. And that's the thing nobody could ever forget, the damn rainbow.

"My husband died for me, you know," Rebecca would tell people. "I dreamt my own death and my husband went instead. Because he knew the children needed me. Because of the children." Now here she was saying it to Alice in her own kitchen.

Alice had no idea what to say. She wasn't at all sure what was real and what was imagined. "He knew the children would suffer. So he died for me. He took my place." Alice could see David, out of the corner of her eye. He had come back into the kitchen, and he was watching, but he wasn't watching Alice.

"I'm so sorry," Alice said. "That must have been very hard for you."

After that, they tried, Rebecca and David, to dispatch Alice to the back porch with the children to peel the apples. "Come on," said Alice, in a voice that rang with common sense. "I really don't think peeling apples is the best job for the children." But she ended up sounding like a schoolmarm and they poo-pooed it and got out some vegetable peelers and a paring knife and swept the children up into the idea, and off Alice went, stuck out there for more than an hour, scared to death that, if she left, one of the children would cut a finger off.

Then, when it came time to assemble the pies, she excused herself. Went upstairs. For a time, she could hear them all laughing and baking. Finally, they settled into the living room when the pies were in the oven. She could hear them making a fire, bringing the logs in from the back. She lay there, on her bed, wondering what she would do now without David. Because, although it was many months before he left, never acknowledging that there was anything at all going on with this woman, Alice knew on that day what was happening, and by his distance, where it would go. So she went downstairs, no longer caring what she did or said, and while the pies were still in the oven, she sent Tobias to his room. ("Why, Mom. I didn't do anything," he protested.) She walked over to Rebecca, sitting next to her husband on the floor in front of the fire, drinking a cup of hot apple cider, and said simply: "Get out of my house."

Rebecca rose slowly, without even looking at Alice, and put on her various scarves and felt hat and droopy chenille sweater. Then she called out to Adrian and, holding him by the hand, moved toward the front door without a word, shaking her head as if she had been insulted for some indiscretion that she couldn't possibly imagine.

"That was unnecessary," David said after Rebecca had left. He told Alice she was crazy, that she was imagining things. He used words like "ridiculous" and "neurotic" to explain away her behavior and said nothing of his own.

That night, David slept on the sofa and Alice slept alone, cradling herself. The next morning, when night was just creeping away, he crawled into bed behind her, naked, and put his arm around her waist, rubbing his chest against her bare back. He kissed her on her right shoulder. "You overreacted," he said. "You know that you overreacted, don't you?"

She lay still, feeling the warmth of his body. "I hope I overreacted," she said softly, sleepily.

"Admit it," he said, reaching under her nightgown and rubbing her stomach. "Admit it: you were jealous." She could smell the smell of him. "Of course I was jealous," she said, turning slowly on her pillow, awakening from the inside out. He was smiling, smiling a wily smile, a teasing kind of smile. As she turned, he reached his arm around her body and ran his right hand across the small of her back and down her flesh to her upper thigh. Everything about him was confident and certain and firm, and she was like flubber bouncing around inside. And the only thing in the world she wanted was to hold him and taste him and finally to lie still beside him. And she wanted to stay like that forever.

CHAPTER 4

Alice & David
1970

Alice met David in 1970, the summer following her eighteenth birthday. She was little more than a child. Long-legged and swift, she had just outgrown three seasons of championship swimming on the county team, distinguishing herself by doing the 100-meter freestyle in record time. Her stroke itself possessed such economy and speed that people came to the meets for no reason other than to watch her in motion. She was languid and smooth. It was as if she could swim in her sleep.

But by the summer of 1970 she knew it was time to give it up. She had graduated from high school the preceding spring, and during her senior year, she had grown her hair long for the first time in her life and taken to wearing it braided down her back, which made her look less like a tomboy and more like a hippie. That June, when the season began, her coach had instructed her to cut it off, insisting that it would slow her down in the water. But that was not what Alice had in mind.

Like other girls of her generation, she had taken to reading feminist writers like Simone de Beauvoir and Germaine Greer. After she read *The Diaries of Anaïs Nin*, she began to picture herself not necessarily as liberated but as something of a libertine, although she liked the idea of it more than she aspired to actually live it. Alice knew damn well, you didn't find many libertines in the lap lanes at the Lancaster County club team pool. By the age of eighteen, she had developed an interest in politics, and she had tried marijuana and flirted with the idea of becoming an actress. She had slept with a junior at the nearby Teacher's College, and he had introduced her to ideas that made the small town in Pennsylvania where she'd grown up seem insulated and pedestrian and, well, small. It wasn't that Alice didn't fit in. It was that she didn't care to fit in. Swimming didn't do it for her anymore. She started playing the piano again.

Her parents had watched this transformation with patience and then concern and, finally, with alarm when she began talking about abandoning her plans for college and moving to New York to pursue a career in theater.

"Dear," her mother had said one night, quite sensibly, when things threatened to blow, "you have never set foot on a stage in your life. I think you're just looking for drama and romance, and you will find it without becoming an actress, I can assure you." Her sisters, she reminded Alice, had found all the excitement they might need at the university. Her father had shouted, "What do you think you're going to live on in New York, young lady? Do you think we're going to pay for this little adventure? Are you going to live in the streets? Then what are you going to do? Brush your teeth with your finger?" And he had stuck his forefinger under his upper lip and rubbed on his gums like a maniac, as if the harder he rubbed the more likely he was to convince her.

Alice sat there quietly, twisting her braid in one hand, surprised by their reaction—particularly the curious comment about the teeth—because she had always imagined that she could do whatever she wanted. It never occurred to her that the idea was far-fetched or that the leap from championship swimmer to struggling actress would be a hard thing to do or that it would be something that her parents would have difficulty accepting. But they did, so she didn't.

She spent that summer filled with a curious mixture of resentment and excitement, working in a Buster Brown shoe factory not far from home, stringing the laces in children's shoes and boxing them up, sitting at a long fold-out table in the middle of a warehouse in Lancaster County with a handful of underemployed adults and long-haired teenagers with bad skin and stringy hair because her parents thought it was time she got a healthy dose of reality. She'd given up her boyfriend and pot and the swimming and her first real dream, which she had decided, after the little talk with her parents, really was little more than a quest for drama.

Somewhere between the time she gave up the boyfriend and started up with the piano again, she began spending her lunch breaks at Longwood Gardens. Longwood had been part of the estate of a very rich man back in the day that housed an uncommon collection of plants and flowers. When he died, some time in the fifties, the gardens and greenhouses and conservatories had been given over to the public. Alice would drive the mile from the Buster Brown warehouse to the old estate and wander through the bonsai room or the orchid room or the room filled with cactus plants and banana trees. These were not little, claustrophobic greenhouses with foggy windows and narrow pathways and air so thick and humid it was impossible to breathe, but gargantuan rooms all connected to one another in a single, massive building, rooms so luscious they took your breath away, with ceilings that soared out of view and windows as thick as a stack of books and pathways that seemed to Alice to be never ending. She could lose herself in them.

She would pack a bag lunch and picnic on the grounds, then steal fifteen or twenty or even thirty minutes in the greenhouses at Longwood before rushing off to punch back in at the Buster Brown warehouse. She found it enchanting and otherworldly, and it made her feel, somehow, that anything was possible in this beautiful world.

Then she discovered the fountains. On Saturday nights in the summers, Longwood would turn on all the fountains in the formal gardens, and the lights—pink and green and yellow and purple lights—would play off the jets of water, which were as tall as trees lined up in rows among the boxwoods. Music—dramatic Beethoven symphonies full of crescendos and Wagner's *Ride of the Valkyries*, and on July 4, the *1812 Overture* with its big bang at the end—played over loudspeakers positioned all over the grounds so, no matter where you were, you felt as if you were in the middle of it. Later in her life, after she had studied music and become a professor, she would have called the performance itself sentimentalized and the entire experience a pop event. But, on those nights, in the summer of 1970, the fountains leaping into the night sky with every swell in the music, luminescent fans of color dancing in the darkness, she felt inspired and lucid and connected to something beyond Longwood Gardens and the Buster Brown factory and the Lancaster County pool.

So every Saturday night for two months, Alice went all by herself to see the fountains dance. It was not at all an easy thing for her to do. Dressing up dateless Saturday after Saturday, driving the long stretch of highway from home with no one to talk to, she would hunt and peck for a decent radio station and curse the traffic jams on Route One. Finally arriving, she'd have to search for a parking spot, generally a good distance from the gardens, and she'd sit alone in the front seat of her father's car and gobble down a sandwich. Then she'd walk through the parking lot alone amid the couples and children and extended families at dusk toting their lawn chairs and antique quilts and picnic baskets and unopened bottles of wine. It took some deter-mination. Round about five o'clock on Saturdays, she'd always hesitate, imagining herself curled up on the living room sofa with a good book that night, safe in her solitude, her parents in the next room playing bridge with friends or preparing dinner. But somehow, even at eighteen, she knew instinctively that you had to break out of your routine if you were going to experience a little magic. She wouldn't have put it quite that way, though. She might have called it communing with God.

Alice came from good people. They were not Bible thumpers but old-fashioned Methodists who went to church every Sunday morning and every Sunday evening and every Wednesday after dinner. For Alice, soul-searching had begun early and been culti-vated in the company of no one other than herself. She had attended Sunday School and confirmation classes and played the piano for choir practices for as long as she could remember. Church was simply part of her life. And in adolescence, when questions about the existence of God and the soul and the meaning of life had first bubbled up—the big questions that preoccupy any thinking person at that age—she had turned to her parents. She found that she received only the most perfunctory answers—unsatisfactory answers.

"What does it mean," she had wondered out loud at the dinner table one Sunday when she was little more than twelve, "Jesus died for our sins?"

They told her that it meant in order to go to heaven, you had to believe in Jesus.

"But does it mean that God was punishing him for our sinful desires?" she went on. "And does it mean that anyone who doesn't believe in Jesus doesn't go to heaven?" She was earnest and direct and sincere.

"God made his own son human, with all the flaws of a human, and then he took him up to heaven so that we could see there was a heaven, and he opened the doors of heaven to us. It means that if we believe in Jesus, our sins are forgiven and we are welcomed into heaven," said her father, speaking slowly in a patronizing tone.

But it didn't make sense to Alice. What about all the good people who didn't believe in Jesus? Were they doomed to hell forever? All because of Jesus. She knew, even as an adolescent, that answer was too simplistic. Too unfair. It had to have as much to do with how you lived and what you experienced inside yourself and how you treated people as it had to do with whether you believed. In fact, none of the answers her father gave her made sense to her. They seemed twisted and convoluted. So she took it upon herself, as she moved through adolescence and into adulthood, to read about it, and after quite a bit of thought and quite a bit of reading, she settled on the only idea that made any sense to her at all—that the Bible was a story and that when you tried to take it too literally, as her father and her mother and too many of her neighbors seemed to do, it got all jumbled up and somehow lost its true meaning. She began to move away from the Church and from her own community and found comfort in solitude.

She turned to books and looked inward for answers. And she looked elsewhere for meaning. Once, not long after she had gotten her first period, she broke away from her family during a Methodist retreat in Bucks County to walk along the Brandywine River, and on a promontory overlooking the river, it had occurred to her with stunning force that she could bear children, that she could create a life, and no matter what else she did, she would have done something of value. It was an epiphany that changed her entire perspective on her life. From that point onward, she wanted nothing more than to find a husband and make a family. Until then, she had seemed content to spend her time alone. She sought out places where she could find comfort, even if it was inconvenient, even if she had to force herself. That summer, Longwood became just such a place.

One night in July of 1970, she prettied herself up and drove to Longwood for the fountain display. That's when she met David. He was in architecture school at the time, six years her senior, and he had driven down from Philadelphia with a date. Alice was dressed in a little print summer dress, something that revealed the muscle tone in her shoulders and her deep cleavage. She looked tall and lean and fit and free, with her auburn hair sliding down her back in a single, long braided strand. She was wearing dangling silver earrings that caught the light from the fountains and glittered with the slightest movement of her head, and she sat on the edge of a low stone wall with no one else. He slipped away from his date and flirted with her and got her number and wrote his name down on a slip of paper so she would remember when he called, which he did.

"I want to see you again" was the last thing he said before he slipped back to his date in the darkness. "And I want to see a lot of you." She found him terribly handsome and romantic and bold, and, dazzled by the fountains and the summer air, she thought that she had met her Prince Charming and fell in love instantly.

At one point, after they'd been out a few times, David and Alice went back to Longwood and spent the day walking through the gardens. They lay in the afternoon grass and just held each other, half napping, their skin electrified, their bodies heating up. They had talked for endless hours, but they hadn't yet kissed.

Looking up at the sky, she asked dreamily, "Do you believe in heaven?"

"This is heaven," he said. Then he explained that Jews didn't really believe in heaven, not the way Christians did. "We believe in making the most of our lives, and the rest—the part about the afterlife, that's really an individual thing. When I was about—I don't know—young, maybe twelve or thirteen, my father told me he didn't believe in God. That there is no proof. That God was invented by man and religion is the opiate of the masses and all that. You know, the whole idea that it's based on fear. One fear or another. Fear of our own mortality, mostly. I think that discussion shaped my perspective on religion. But now I don't know what I believe."

Then David had talked about Judaism and the importance of ritual. About his bar mitzvah and how his father hadn't been there. "He didn't even show up. By then, he and my mother were divorced, and he just didn't care," David had said. "I never want to be like my father." She was saddened by it, but mesmerized, fascinated by this strange man from this other world.

After that, they drove to a rundown old bar in an asbestos-clad house on the edge of some working-class neighborhood in Philadelphia. They smoked cigarettes and played pool and drank whisky. She was the only woman in the place, filled with unshaven men in overalls and work shirts. She felt sexy and seedy. He tried to make her laugh.

"What's redneck foreplay?" he asked, watching her face, gauging her reaction to the word. *Foreplay.* She braced herself, not knowing what to expect, afraid that she wouldn't get the joke. He leaned over the pool table and took a smooth shot, making it easily, and then, taking his time, slid over, right up next to her, waiting for her answer.

"Redneck foreplay," he said again. Then he nudged her with his elbow and said, "Hey—you awake?" She laughed. The men, with their big bellies and dirty hands, had all looked at her. David didn't seem to notice them. She was only slightly aware of how she looked to them. Beautiful young women know they have power. But they don't really know how much until they get older, and they lose it. Then they look back and envy their own sexuality and know the true measure of its value. If she was uncomfortable, she didn't let on. She maintained her bravado, laughing too loud, drawing their attention, although she didn't mean to. David threw ten dollars down on the bar. "Let's go," he said. And they went back to his apartment.

Her parents were relieved and pleased and greeted him warmly when he came by the house a few weeks later and every night, it seemed, after that. He would take her to his apartment near the university, night after night, where they would wrestle about and screw and talk and laugh, and that was the summer she learned about her body and what it could do and what a man could do. That, with just a few words and a brush of his hand, David could make her spirit leap. He made her feel free, but she wasn't. She was caught up in him.

They were in school, together really, both at the University of Pennsylvania, the next year and then the next, until she found out he'd been sleeping with other women, because he made sure she found out—by leaving things around his apartment like telephone numbers and condoms and underpants that didn't belong to her. So she left him, crushed and bereft and feeling betrayed, and thinking she would never love anyone again. Not long afterward, he finished graduate school and went off to New York to get a job.

She had, partially in defiance of her parents and partially out of an evolving love for it, taken up music. It lacked the drama and engagement and community of theater, but in it she found an expression for the side of her that needed to grow. What she lacked in talent, she made up for in determination and interest, and though she was only a passable pianist, she had a good ear, and she could listen to music for hours on end. She became intrigued by music history and music theory and the makers of music—great composers, great musicians. She became a music major and, when she graduated, decided to give piano lessons at a nearby school. She was adrift somewhere between college and adulthood, uncertain of where exactly she was headed.

She became a kind of groupie, picking up local jazz musicians in bars in Philadelphia and folk singers at coffee houses. Although she couldn't quite bring herself to sleep with any of them, she would flirt with them and drink and talk for endless hours, while they explored her with their eyes thinking that the evening held something that it did not hold at all. That is how she spent her early twenties: teaching piano and flirting with local musicians.

After a while, she grew restless. Like many women of her generation, as independent as she imagined herself to be, she couldn't quite become an adult until she had a husband. It was as if she couldn't really move on without some kind of anchor. She took little pleasure in her students or her companions and fell into wondering what she was going to do with the rest of her life. That, of course, was precisely when David came back into the picture, with pleas of forgiveness and promises of fidelity.

They married, because she believed him, knowing that he was the love of her life and imagining a future full of kisses and ideas and babies.

CHAPTER 5

Alice & David
Summer 1984

My albatross. That's what he called the backwash from his peccadilloes at the university years before and the mistrust that it kindled in Alice in the beginning, when they were first married. And once, just to tease, to bedevil her, he'd said facetiously, "I guess it's the cross that I must bear." Those were the words he used when it surfaced on occasion in those early years.

"How did you two meet?" someone would ask, when David was introducing her to his colleagues at the office or to new people at some social event. And that would get it started. Instead of giving them the safe answer, the easy answer—"We met at Longwood Gardens"—David would tell them they'd been college sweethearts, although not technically, he would say. "Actually, I was in graduate school." And they'd explain that they'd split up and he'd moved to Manhattan, that he'd come back for her five years later and proposed. "Couldn't live without her," David would always say. And everyone thought it was so romantic. But Alice always thought that if he'd gone ahead and told the whole story, the real story, well, it wasn't so terribly romantic.

So, in truth, it was their Roshamon. Because, later, when they'd get back home, he'd say, "You just left me without a word," or even, "You broke my heart," or to be particularly melo-dramatic, he'd say that she had plunged him into despair. "That's so twisted," she'd say. "I didn't just up and leave you. You were cheating on me." And he'd explain it away by saying "I was so young" or "We weren't even married at the time" or, sometimes, that he loved her more than anyone in the world and wanted to sleep with Alice, and only Alice, for the rest of his life. And these discussions always ended in the same way, with his arms around her and his kisses on her neck.

During the years in Manhattan after they first married, there were many nights when David didn't come home until two or three in the morning. She'd confront him, directly and unashamedly. And always he'd say: "I was at the office" and "Are you never going to trust me?" and then, finally, in frustration, "It's like a fucking albatross." Until, finally, one night, he was gone all night long, although he'd called and explained about this project for the Belfords and how they kept changing their minds and they were driving everyone insane, and he was going to have to pull an all-nighter. But she didn't believe him. So the next day, he called her from his office, and he put two other architects on the line and then his boss. And, yes, they all confirmed it, yes, they'd all been at the office all night working on the Belford apartment. "They're a pain in the ass," said David's boss. Then Alice got a reputation for being jealous crazy-woman and it became kind of a joke around his office even though, after that, she stopped asking and stopped confronting him. Because, that night he made some joke about "the cross that I must bear," and then, very seriously, he got down on his knees and held her by the hands and said: "I promise. I promise I will never, ever be unfaithful to you. You are my wife. And I love you. And I promise it won't happen. So please stop." And when she did, the whole issue seemed to dissipate.

But, out of nowhere—from Alice's perspective, at least—it surfaced again, in the summer of 1984. Seven years into their marriage. The albatross. That was the year they went to Italy. Alice called it their last summer. Their last summer of freedom. Their last summer before real life, because they were going to leave New York. They had bought a house in Washington, D.C. —a real house, they both proclaimed, astonished at themselves— and she'd gotten a teaching position at Georgetown University, and he was going to open his own office there. And then, of course, there would be children. It was all settled.

Before the move, they spent six weeks in Italy, a break for both of them. He got a position at Cornell's architecture program in Rome, teaching a design studio. She linked up with a professor at the American Academy in Rome to study composition. And, although they did their work, there was a frenzy to the summer.

More than anything else, it was a summer of intense play— of road trips and picnics and late nights and elaborate al fresco feasts with the raucous American faculty in Rome. They drank too much and ate too much and made love with a reckless passion—outdoors and in their miniscule rental car on the roadside near Orvieto and, once, on a Sunday, in his design studio when there was no one else around. They seemed to be approaching the future the way a bachelor approaches his wedding day—with a combination of excitement and dread, of taking on and letting go.

One night, in the midst of it, he turned to her and said simply: "I don't know if I can do this anymore." They were sitting at an outdoor café not far from the Spanish Steps sipping aperitifs, doing nothing more than watching the passersby, when a girl approached their table, a pretty girl in sandals and a little slip of a dress. "Professor," she had said, startling them. He was quite obviously taken aback. "Janice," he said. He was friendly enough but stiffened slightly and didn't introduce Alice.

Janice seemed hardly able to contain herself. "I can't believe I ran into you. I've just come from the studio. Your idea—I incorporated it into the design. It's brilliant. Everything about it works." She was awkward, holding a notebook against her half-exposed breasts and standing there very still, waiting for some kind of response, which, for some unknown reason David elected to withhold. Finally, he spoke. "Good. Good. We'll talk about it tomorrow" was all he said. "I just wanted to thank you," she bubbled. "I mean, I certainly didn't expect to see you. I didn't mean to interrupt." She was apologetic then, looking at David and Alice. She said I'm sorry two or three times, and David said something formal and professorial like "I'll look forward to seeing what you've done with it." And she disappeared back into the crowd.

Alice knew not to ask questions like "Who was that?" or say anything like "She's lovely," anything that might imply that David was attracted to her—because it would raise the albatross. She certainly wouldn't have asked anything as simple as "Why didn't you introduce me?" Because she knew exactly what he'd say: "She's just a student." Or "I don't even remember her last name." And that could be true, she thought.

After this Janice, this girl in the little slip dress, had walked away, they sat in silence for a time. It was just a student, Alice thought. But apparently, that was not what David imagined she was thinking, or maybe that's not what David himself was thinking.

"I don't know if I can do this anymore," he said. She didn't know what he meant.

"What? Teach?" she replied. But that's not what he meant.

"Be married. I don't know if I can do it anymore."

"What are you talking about?" she said. It had all seemed so perfect to her. The time in Rome. Their place in Manhattan. And now, now they were going to move to Washington, D.C. He was going to start his own practice. He already had a client. They had talked about having children. It didn't make sense.

"It just feels so suffocating sometimes."

"Where did this come from?"

"Just now. I mean, what I really wanted to do was go back to the studio and see that girl's work."

"Yeah."

"And I didn't."

"Yeah."

"Because of you. Because I thought it would upset you. Because you'd think it was something that it wasn't."

"And you'd what? Give up our marriage because of that?"

"But it happens all the time. I just feel like I can't give you what you want."

She was upset then. "What I want? It sounds to me like this is about what you want. What makes you think I would have cared if you went to the studio? You can't do this anymore? Isn't this what we're supposed to do in a marriage—talk about it."

"That's the problem. You're so caught up in what we're supposed to do." He was getting angry.

"Is this about having children?"

"Jesus, Alice. That's all you ever think about."

She got angry then. Got up from the table and stormed off

toward home by herself, but it wasn't home at all. It was a borrowed studio off some strange, narrow, stone-covered street in a city that wound around in circles. She still didn't know it very well. And she'd gotten lost, wandering about frightened and upset. It took her an hour to find her way, and by the time she arrived he was already there, pacing and nervous and worried.

"Don't ever do that again. Please don't ever do that again," he had cried when she came through the door. "I thought I'd lost you." He was dramatic and romantic and the whole thing was hopelessly overblown. When they left Italy, they both went on as if it had never happened.

CHAPTER 6

Alice & Friends
November 1996

"Maybe I'm losing my mind." That is what Alice was beginning to think, so she set up dinner with her two closest friends, because she hadn't a clue anymore what was real and what was imagined. She knew she could trust them, trust their judgment, trust them to shake her out of it. They'd each been married for years. Howard had been her mentor, her ally at the university; she wasn't at all sure she would have gotten tenure if it hadn't been for Howard. And Pam had been her friend forever. She wasn't looking forward to it, though. To telling them. She had the feeling that once you began to share the intimate details of your marriage with other people, once you put your suspicions out there for all the world to see, then the marriage must surely be doomed. But what choice do I have, she'd asked herself. One of the other mothers from The School had asked her outright, "How is everything with you and David?" That was not long after that awful day with the apples and the pies and Rebecca and the children. She'd had coffee with the woman—Delia was her name—at Delia's invitation. They'd run into one another in the halls one morning after Alice had dropped Toby off at his classroom ("Please, escort your children to their classrooms every day," read The Handbook), and she'd run into Delia.

Delia was thin and rich and chic, with very close-cropped blond hair and creamy skin, and Alice couldn't imagine why she'd put her two overdressed children in this hippie school. Most of the kids wore cast-off clothes, and all of them—parents, teachers and children—were a bit like refugees from the sixties. "Sandal-schleppers," Howard called them when he went with her once, to pick up Tobias. On Family Day, when Alice's entire family had come because David really didn't have a family, her mother had asked why so many of the teachers were Amish, and, afterward, her sister Catherine had said, "Now that was a pretty heavy quotient of weirdos." And Sarah, an English teacher who had always been the most sensible of the three sisters and had been particularly curious about the place, raised serious questions about the curriculum, calling it bizarre. Toby was learning to knit, his classroom teacher had explained, and by third grade, he would be able to start reading—because, according to The Handbook, a child shouldn't be expected to learn to read until all his or her teeth had come in. "What's that all about?" Sarah had asked Alice later. "I've seen Tobias read."

But, at the time, Alice had defended The School, defended all of it, suggesting that maybe it was wise to have an open mind. Catherine had said, "Sure, but not so open that your brains fall out."

And now Alice was beginning to think they were right. What had seemed at first like a haven for Toby was beginning to feel like something insidious—a community that was a little bit too close-knit, too prescriptive, too rigid. The Handbook was their Bible, and even mild dissent was, well, frowned upon, unwelcome, discouraged. You had to fit in. And Alice didn't.

Delia seemed a bit more mainstream than the others. Her husband was a real estate developer and something of a local heavyweight. He and David had become fast friends. More than once in the past few months, David had said he'd miss dinner because he was having a drink with Steve. "Who the hell is Steve?" Alice had asked the first time. "You know, the developer. From The School." "Oh, yeah, of course, Steeeeve," Alice had said flippantly. She knew him only as Stephen Banks. In fact, she didn't know him at all.

But, of course, that had been happening for nearly a year now. David had started picking up new people. A few weeks into the school year, he'd invited a couple over for dinner, a sculptor and his wife, without mentioning a word about it to Alice. "Don't worry. I'll cook something up," he'd said off-handedly. The woman was some kind of masseuse. "I do healing through massage," she said. "She does Reiki," her husband explained. "It's totally radical. Great for headaches." But when Alice had asked a couple of questions—like "How does it work?" and "What do you do?"—the woman was dismissive. "Ask your husband," she said. "He knows all about it." And she turned away from Alice and back to David.

"Where on earth did you find them?" Alice asked afterward. Turned out they had a child in the eighth grade at The School.

And he'd started hanging out at Tisha's, a hip new coffee shop near DuPont Circle where they made espresso and fresh-baked bread and served paninis for lunch. He'd go there every morning before he went into the office and on Saturdays. He'd become one of the regulars. A couple of times she met him down there in the afternoon when she got a break in her schedule at school. He knew all the other regulars and he'd invite them over to the table to join the two of them. Alice and David had always had their own lives, their own work, and friends of their own, but all of it orbited around their marriage. Now it had begun to feel as if the marriage itself was no longer at the center. Alice couldn't put her finger on it, but something wasn't quite right.

That year, on David's birthday, he'd planned an evening out with a handful of the regulars from Tisha's, people Alice had never even met. They were an odd crew: a stand-up comedian in his mid-thirties, a volunteer firefighter, a divorce lawyer who must have been sixty, and a spindly young woman who taught jazz dance. They didn't seem to have a thing in common except Tisha's. Otherwise, they seemed hopelessly disconnected—no husbands or wives, no children, and they'd all recently moved to Washington from somewhere else. Alice had made dinner reservations weeks before at David's favorite restaurant, and she'd invited a couple of their old friends, but David had insisted that she cancel. "I just want to do something different," he'd said. So the six of them went to a bar on upper Wisconsin Avenue that served half-assed food, and the people from Tisha's treated her as if she was, well, expendable. They didn't say anything nice and embracing when they met her, like "I'm so glad to finally meet you" or "We've heard so much about you." But, of course, neither did she.

One Saturday afternoon in early October some kid pulled up in front of the house on a motorcycle and said he was there to pick up David. But David wasn't home. "Just have him call me, wouldja?" the young man had said, setting his motorcycle helmet back on top of his head and giving her his card. That and the Reiki woman and the little run-in with Delia were jarring, coming in the wake of Rebecca's visit to the house. Her encounter with Delia suggested that everyone at The School was somehow in on it, that they all knew something was awry in Alice's marriage.

Delia fairly gushed when she saw Alice that morning at school, although Alice barely knew her: "I never see you." She stretched out the word "never" in a contrived, Hollywood kind of way. They went to a little place around the corner where people sat on top of one another, an organic grocery store that was cold and impersonal, oddly placed in a nearby strip mall, with white Formica tables and little boxes of tea on the shelves, and rows and rows of vitamins. There were a couple of other parents from The School there, stocking up on organic goods. Alice was self-conscious, uncomfortable, imagining that they could hear every word she said.

"Stephen is driving me crazy with this little plot that he and David are hatching," Delia began, referring to her husband, the developer. Alice, of course, had no idea what she was talking about. It apparently had something to do with The School, raising money and building some kind of pavilion, an arts center, a place to display the children's work and for dramatic productions and concerts. They'd formed a committee and planned some sort of meeting at their house—Delia and Stephen's—that Sunday. "And I'm supposed to go shopping for this little diversion," Delia said. Alice knew nothing of it. And then Delia began to twist the conversation around, turning it to Rebecca and how she was involved in some way, "because she's such an integral part of The School," she said. "And so creative." She added something about Stephen and Rebecca, off-handedly—"I think my Stephen has a little crush on her," she said. "I'm sure all the fathers do," she added. And then she dropped in the question about Alice's marriage. "Is everything okay with you and David?" Only, at first, Alice assumed she was just asking about whether they were both okay, about how they were doing. Delia must know about Jeremiah, she thought. And then, she reasoned, of course she does. So she answered simply, "We're doing a lot better." And then Alice said something like, "It's been a few rough years, but I think we're past the worst of it." But, from the expression on Delia's face, it became clear that the woman had no idea what Alice was talking about. A few rough years. And then Alice realized that this woman she hardly knew had been asking something else altogether.

She'd been asking whether everything was okay between the two of them, between David and Alice. And then, when Alice checked her watch and insisted that she had to get to class, Delia put her hand on Alice's arm, forcing an intimacy that didn't exist, and said firmly: "Listen to me, honey. When you're not lovin' your man, you're asking for trouble."

Alice called Pam and Howard the next day. She needed to see her old friends. She needed a reality check. The holiday season was approaching. That was her excuse: "Let's get together before things get insane," she had told them both.

They chose a new Italian place down near the Canal. Howard chose it, actually. It wasn't far from the university, and, since the death of his partner a few years before, Howard had been spending most of his time at school, hiding, working. Alice feared that he was lonely and worried about him, probably more than she needed to. He looked like an old sea captain, and everyone was crazy about him, because he was wise and charming and good-natured and handsome. She saw him every day at school. Pam was busy, at home with five children, and Alice hadn't seen her in months.

The restaurant was cavernous. The faux marble walls had a rusty orange cast to them, which gave the meandering space a dank, musty feel. It was half-empty, couples mostly, drinking red wine, huddled over small round tables. They ordered drinks.

Cosmopolitans all around. After they'd surveyed the menu for a good ten minutes, Pam and Howard got into a congratulatory exchange about the presidential election that had just passed. Alice listened in silence.

"What on earth is the matter with you?" Pam said finally, after the two of them had spent a good ten minutes raking Bob Dole over the coals. "Are you not speaking this evening?" And Alice told them, carefully, tentatively at first. "Something's wrong. Something's wrong with David. I don't know." She was tearing up. They prodded and cajoled—"Like what?" and "What's the matter with him?" and "Oh God, he's not sick, is he? "No, no, no," she answered emphatically, reassuringly. "It's not that." She told them that he just didn't seem like himself. That he seemed distant and preoccupied. "And he's gotten really involved in Tobias's school."

"Well, that's not a bad thing," said Pam.

"I don't know. I'm not too crazy about the place at the moment," Alice said, and she struggled to explain it using words like "cultish" and "doctrinaire" and "touchy-feely" and "not terribly rigorous academically." Pam said, "I thought that's what you wanted. A place where Toby could feel safe and secure." And Alice started to say that it was really David who seemed to find the place safe and secure, that he seemed to take comfort in it. And that it was almost as if the school was the extended family that he'd never had.

But Howard jumped in and told a story about some Georgetown faculty member who'd taken her daughter out of that place because of *Sesame Street*. "Alice, you must know her," he said. "Francis McCracken. Irish Studies. A real maternal type. Kinda flaky, but sharp as a whip."

"What about *Sesame Street*?" Pam interrupted.

Howard explained that some teacher had confronted this

Francis McCracken about letting her daughter watch *Sesame Street*, and she was furious, and she had pulled her daughter out of class and never went back.

"They don't allow TV," said Alice.

"They don't allow it?" Pam said. And Howard said: "Right. And I'd like to know what else they're monitoring. Whether you serve organic vegetables in sufficient quantities? Your sex life? Whether your language is appropriate?"

"Then I'm in big trouble," Alice said. And they all laughed. "Here's what got me. I asked Toby's teacher last month about the possibility of getting some kind of after-school program in place —and she told me that they don't approve of after-school programs."

"Well, I can see that," said Pam. "I mean, these kids spend enough time at school."

"Maybe so, but most schools offer after-school care. I've got a three o'clock class to teach every Tuesday next semester. And I don't know what I'm going to do."

Howard was genuinely concerned. And she told him she'd written a letter to the board of The School to see if she could work on putting a program in place. "If not, it wouldn't be such a big deal," she said. "It's only one afternoon a week. And David could pick Tobias up." But that wasn't really what had upset her, she explained. It was the teacher's response that had upset her. "Maybe you should think about staying home," she'd said, as if Alice were doing something wrong. "I mean, what am I supposed to do, quit my job so I can pick Tobias up at school one afternoon a week? I mean, jeez, I pick him up every day as it is."

"A wee bit judgmental, wouldn't you say?" said Howard. "I'd pull a Francis McCracken. I'd get him out of there."

"Alice, don't push it," said Pam. "Toby's been through enough changes."

"I don't think he's that happy there. And David's all wrapped up in the place. And I just feel kind of alienated from the whole thing. I feel like I suddenly woke up and found myself in the middle of a nightmare." And then, finally, Alice said, "And there's this woman. This parent. I don't know. They're working on some project together. She and David. Some pavilion."

"He's having an affair," Pam said matter-of-factly.

"That's absurd," said Howard. "Honey, he adores her." Then, turning to Alice. "He does."

But Alice could hardly make sense of it herself. David continued to dismiss her concerns. "You have nothing to worry about," he'd say. And when he was around, they made love now with such intensity and such frequency that it almost frightened her. But his touch had changed. In some indefinable way, he felt different. In bed, like any couple that had been married for more than a few years, they were like actors in a set piece who repeat the same lines over and over, night after night, week after week; then, when all of a sudden, one of the actors changes his tone even slightly or moves about the stage with a bit of twist, the audience doesn't know the difference, but the people in the cast know. Alice knew. It was unmistakable. But she didn't tell Howard and Pam all that.

"I don't know," Alice said. "He says it's nothing."

By the time they'd finished their cosmopolitans and the main course and polished off a bottle of red wine, and they'd talked about a dozen other subjects—Pam's children and Howard's love life and more politics—Pam and Howard turned their attention back to David. They decided that they needed dessert. That Alice needed something rich and chocolaty, so they ordered a tiramisu with three forks. And then they wanted to know more about Rebecca and who she was, anyway. They wanted details.

"Hmm," Howard said. "Sounds like she might be considered sexy." But then he recanted, apologizing profusely in the face of Pam's glare and the positively crushed look on Alice's face.

When the tiramisu arrived, they were well into their second bottle of wine, and they'd made a game of it. How to catch him in the act. Or how to devise some trick that would send Rebecca running. "I know a woman," Pam said conspiratorially, "who suspected her husband of having an affair, so she invited the other woman out to lunch and befriended her. She shamed her into dropping the whole thing without even saying a word about it. I think it was brilliant."

"Oh, perfect! You could just invite her to dinner." Howard was positively gleeful. "She's a widow, you say? Invite me. I'll be the fourth. We'll make a party of it."

"We'll put strychnine in her cassoulet!" cried Pam.

"We'll stab her with the bread knife!" said Alice.

"Yes. Yes. Yes," exclaimed Howard. "Colonel Mustard in the observatory with the candlestick!"

By the end of the evening, they were laughing, all of them. Even Alice was laughing. Before they said goodnight, they'd decided that she should just ride the thing out. That it had been a rough few years, after all.

"Four years," said Alice.

"Well, you've both been through the hardest thing in the world together," Howard said. And he said that she should be patient, because everyone knew they loved each other and that they were such a good couple. "Sounds like some mid-life thing," said Pam. "Isn't he almost fifty?" They hugged her and told her they loved her and said, "Let's do this again soon. Before the new year. Promise?" By the time she arrived home, Alice felt better, reassured by the tone of the evening and comforted by their affection and humor. She'd also had a good bit of wine to soften her edges.

When she came through the front door, she found Tobias and David sitting quietly in the living room playing chess. They'd put on some classical guitar music. It was soft and gentle and melodic, but she wasn't sure she'd ever heard it before. They had a fire going, and the room felt warm and civilized. Toby was winning and David was basking in it. "My son, the chess wizard," he said. He had very nearly consumed an entire bottle of wine, and sitting next to it on the table was a list.

"We've got it all planned," said Toby, picking up the list and waving it in the air. "Dad's going to make his stuffing."

"Oyster stuffing," said David, grinning.

"And I'm going to make the pumpkin pie," Toby went on, excited, holding up the list. "With Dad, of course. And look, all you have to do is make the turkey and one vegetable, because didn't you say Aunt Catherine was going to bring those sweet potatoes with the marshmallows? And Grandmom is bringing her coleslaw."

"Sounds like a plan," she said. Sounds like our family, our rituals. Sounds like our old life, she was thinking.

Alice sidled up on the sofa next to David. He was still bent over the chessboard, and she rubbed his back gently. And she started to relax, to let her guard down. She watched as they finished up the game, languishing in it. Then, when Toby got up and gathered up the chess pieces, she was thinking they would stay there for a time—all three of them, there in the living room with the wine and the fire and the music. But David announced that it was time for Toby to go ahead and get ready for bed.

Once he'd gone, they sat, the two of them, and finished off the wine. And Alice opened up about The School—about

Tobias. That he didn't seem terribly happy there—and that she wasn't so sure it was the right place for him, for them. And about the whole question of what she was going to do on Tuesday afternoons and what the teacher had said. David didn't seem terribly comfortable with the conversation, and he listened more than he talked. But when he did start talking, he said things that didn't make any sense to Alice, crazy things, things that she would never have imagined he was thinking. And he used a measured tone of voice, calm and quiet, as if he'd given all these matters a great deal of thought. It was a patronizing tone.

"Maybe you should think about staying home," he said. "I think it might be healthier." He'd been thinking about the tic. Toby's tic. Someone at school had recommended an acupuncturist and maybe that would work. "What do you think? Because it's obviously nerve related. He needs to calm his nerves, and that's what acupuncture's for." When Alice said she had no intention of giving up her job, that it was important to her, important to them, and that Toby was nine years old and surely, he could go to David's office one afternoon a week or go over to Pam's house or something, he said, "But she lets them watch TV. And you know how we feel about TV." And then, in what seemed like a sudden burst of insight, he perked up and suggested that maybe Toby could go to Rebecca's on Tuesday afternoons, because Rebecca knew what she was doing. In fact, he said, maybe she could take him home every day, if that would make things easier for Alice. Maybe Rebecca could take Toby home every day. "I'm sure she'd be happy to do it," he said. Alice couldn't speak. She was unwilling to shatter the glow of the room and the afterglow of her evening with Howard and Pam.

David got up and stoked the fire. They had turned the lights off and the CD had stopped, so the room had grown very dark and quiet. He looked up at her, the light from the fire dancing across his face, and he said, almost innocently, "Alice, let's have another baby." And he was too far away to touch, too far away for her to reach him, but she wanted to have her arms around him when she said it. She wanted to hold him when she answered, but he had that poker in his hand, and he was chipping away at a log, and she would have had to climb over the coffee table to get to him. So she said, from across the room, as gently as she could, "Honey, I'm forty-four years old."

It occurred to her then that Toby had gone up to get ready for bed, but no one had gone to say goodnight. No one had tucked him in or turned off his light. "I need to put Toby to bed," she said and left the room.

CHAPTER 7

David & Alice
1984

David did everything with a passion and nothing with certainty. He'd latch on to what he wanted or what he loved—an idea or a person or a building or a book—with great intensity and then, if he had a moment's doubt about it, he'd threaten to abandon it altogether, often with some grand proclamation—like the time in Italy when he announced that he just couldn't do it anymore, couldn't be married. Or the time, a few months before Toby was born, when he proclaimed over dinner that he wasn't ready to have children, as if they could somehow take it back. Even though he had been passionate about having a baby. Yet, after Toby was born, David would jump up in a panic at the slightest whimper. Once, when Toby was about two weeks old, the child sneezed a couple of times and it sent David into a tailspin. He got the doctor on the phone, even though it was something like ten o'clock on a Sunday night. "Hey, relax," Alice had said. "It's only a sneeze, for God's sake." It was hard for Alice to know from one day to the next how David might react to something, but she was always certain that he would react. Sometimes—when he'd come up with some cockamamie idea—she would try to steer him back to his center, but usually he'd find his way back himself after a few days or even a few minutes.

He was a dreamer. It was just hard sometimes to predict precisely what form his dreams would take. And that was one of the things she loved about him.

By his dreams, David had shaped her. He was her mentor, her inspiration. When they first married and she joined him in New York, he was working for an edgy young firm that did steely interiors for lofts in SoHo and rehabs on the Upper West Side. And he seemed excited by it, excited by everything. On weekends, they'd spend their days just walking around, exploring the city's museums and neighborhoods. She gloried in it. David was teaching her about art and architecture and New York. He'd bring his sketchbook along on their treks, and they'd talk about the ideas he was developing, the underpinnings of his designs. "It's all about ritual," he'd say. "It's all about how people live their daily lives." She imagined that she was his muse, although he never said so. And, in truth, it was David who became her muse.

She got a job teaching music at a private school nearby. For the first time, she began composing. She started with songs for the children to sing in class; then, they'd asked her to develop a school production, something for the parents. She called it "The Forest" and made each of the students a forest creature and gave them each melody of their own, rather like *Peter and the Wolf,* and then she wove all the melodies together into a grand finale for all the children. Everyone called it brilliant. "Is this your brilliant teacher?" a mother asked her four-year-old child, who just nodded dumbly. After that, she got more serious about her music.

They lived on West End Avenue, just off 107th, in a small, dreary first-floor apartment with a railroad kitchen, where nearly all the windows were painted shut and covered with burglar bars. They put a little spinet in the spare bedroom, a room barely bigger than a walk-in closet, and she began composing, squeezed between its walls, on nights when David was tied up with his work. She started to develop new pieces, original pieces, drawing on what she knew and what she listened to. Sometimes, he'd come in late and find her there, and she'd play for him. He'd sit right next to her and watch her fingers intently, and her face, and wrap his arm around behind her. He seemed in awe of it. And he became her audience.

They both wanted children—or, at some point, she was certain that he said he did—but they were preoccupied with each other and with their work. Like any young couple that can afford the luxury of it, they spent a fair amount of time trying to figure out where they fit in the world and how they fit with each other and digging into the feast that was outside their doorstep and inside their bedroom.

Alice discovered the Brooklyn Botanic Gardens and The Cloisters, and all the other wonders the city had to offer. Sometimes, after school, she'd just go down to Riverside Park and walk along the Hudson and watch the kids on the playground overlooking the river, a few blocks from her house. They were a ragtag bunch, playing with frantic energy, unleashed from their own cramped apartments. She tried to imagine what it would be like to be one of them or to have children there. But she couldn't. She wanted her kids to have a neighborhood, like she'd had in Lancaster, and a yard and maybe even a dog. She had an idyllic picture of it.

On Sundays, after she and David had come from the Guggenheim or the Metropolitan, they'd walk together through

Central Park and come upon another breed of child—pristine girls in pinafores, and boys in little navy-blue jackets and short pants or old-fashioned aprons; and babies in elaborate strollers, the parents decked out in elegant suits in muted colors. Like the families at her school, but more so. And different from Riverside Park, she'd think. So controlled, those Central Park children seemed. She didn't like the idea. She called them Stepford children. And when she overheard some well-dressed mother reprimanding a child in soft, emotionless tones, saying something like, "That's not okay" in response to a major infraction or creamy-white words like "Please use your indoor voice" in the face of a screaming tantrum, she called them Stepford Moms and was amused by it. So precious, she thought.

On the subway, one day, they saw a small child sobbing uncontrollably as his mother kept thwacking him on the head and saying, "Shut up." Alice pleaded with David to do something, say something. Finally, she'd gone up to the woman and said, "Excuse me. I'm a teacher. And I think you're just upsetting him more," and the woman had looked at her with a stony glare and said, "Mind your business." It had given Alice chills. And she was outraged. "I'm a teacher," David said, laughing, shaking his head when they got off the subway. "You kill me," he said.

Ultimately, it was David who inspired her to apply to NYU, to get an advanced degree, to pursue her music and to become a composer. "You're too good not to," he said one night when he came home and found her at the piano composing a jazzy piece, sort of Gershwin-esque. They'd talked about the structure of music, about the creative process, about how her composing was so much like what he did. "You hear the music in your head," he said. "I see the buildings, the rooms, the architecture in mine."

"Sometimes I feel like all I'm doing is copying," she'd said. "It's not really that original, you know."

He'd bristle at that. "Everything is built on what's come before," he'd say. "That's the process."

And by the time they were ready to leave New York, Alice wasn't Alice anymore. She was a different person, more intellectual, more engaging, and absolutely dedicated to her work, her composing. And it was David, more than anyone else, who had made her what she had become. Her compositions had grown more complex, and she'd grown more confident. One of her pieces had been nominated for a Stoeger Prize, and she was offered a postgraduate fellowship in Oxford, Mississippi, to study the blues—although she'd turned it down ("Too far away," she'd said). David was on the verge of making partner and he'd won some awards as well, national design awards, impressive awards. He was in his late thirties and ready to start his own practice and one of the big clients at his firm offered him a project in Washington, D.C. "I can give you enough business to keep you busy for a year," he'd said. So they had decided to go.

In 1984, seven years after they'd arrived in New York and after she'd finished her degree, and not long before they would leave the city and travel to Italy and then settle in D.C., they went with another couple to the Shubert Theater to see *Sunday in the Park with George*. It so struck them both that the whole thing, in its entirety, became their song, their anthem, the totem of their relationship. In much the same way that another couple might play some love song for each other over and over again at anniversary parties and candlelight dinners, the whole of *Sunday in the Park with George* became theirs.

It was a new show, and it hadn't yet won the Pulitzer Prize, so they felt like they had discovered it all by themselves, together. They were both enthralled with the lyrics and Alice with the score. It was like nothing she'd ever heard before. "It's rapturous," she said, sitting at the bar afterward with the other couple. "How about that piece where he's painting, and the music echoes the sound of the dots he was making with his brush?" she said. She was excited, agitated. And he was excited too. "Pointillism," he said. "Pointillism put to music."

The other couple was less enthusiastic. "Didn't he do *West Side Story*?" said the woman. "It's not at all like *West Side Story*." And her husband, one of David's clients in the financial services industry, said, "It makes everyone who isn't an artist look like a fool" and "I thought it was a bit cerebral." And David looked at Alice, across the table, and silently mouthed the words "I love you." And she said, "Me too." But she said it out loud and the client thought she was talking to him, and he went on and on about how inaccessible it was, looking to her for confirmation, which she never delivered. She and David were smiling at each other and playing footsies under the table.

At that point in their lives, Sondheim's masterpiece seemed to be about everything that mattered to them and everything that was always going to matter to them. About the creative process and the value of art. About originality and how to achieve it and what exactly it is. And about romance. "I love that line about not worrying that what you're doing is new. Did you get that, Alice?" he said. He said it in much the same way a teacher would talk to a student. They went out and bought the tape the next day. Over the years, they'd play it in the car when they took road trips, and he'd play it when he was designing. She bought the score so she could study it. They went to see it again, years later, when it came to the Kennedy Center as part of a Sondheim review.

At first, Alice and David's relationship had been all about chemistry, but in New York, their bond had deepened into something more. And on that night, the night they discovered *Sunday in the Park with George*, they had celebrated that connection.

Once the other couple had left and Alice and David were walking up Broadway, she said: "Did you get the piece about children and art? I loved that. The two most important things. Did you hear that? Children and art." She elbowed him in the side. And he laughed and rolled his eyes.

When they had left New York and they'd been to Italy and moved to Washington and finally had children, David had fallen easily into loving them. And for all those years afterward, there was no albatross. They were so wrapped up in one another, in sharing ideas and raising their children and building a life. She had her composing and teaching, and he, his designing. It took all the energy they had. Every now and then, he'd drop some dream on her—let's move back to New York or let's get a place in the country or let's join a temple. Or let's have another baby. It would always come out of the blue. Sometimes they'd follow it and sometimes not. But, back then, she could always tell where he was headed by the direction of his dreams.

CHAPTER 8

Alice
1997

In the darkness she wakes. Something has stirred in the night. Tobias? The dog? But Hobbes is lying quietly at the foot of the bed. And there are no footsteps in the attic above them where Tobias sleeps now. Unmoving, she listens.

David is lying still beside her, with his back to her. Usually he sleeps fitfully, but not on this night. He's still as a stone. And, feeling him beside her and watching him sleep, she is struck by a night terror. She wraps her arms around his naked body, the body that has given her more pleasure than any other body in the world. And she is filled then with a feeling that is so dark, so unfathomable that she is overwhelmed by it.

She knows that someday he will be gone.

This man with whom she has made a home and plans and babies—this man who has made her life what it is—will not always be there. And she will wake in the night and find herself alone in the darkness. She knows it is the truth. He has gone so far off center that she knows she can't ever reel him back.

She kisses him on the shoulder, gently so as not to wake him. She soaks up the feeling of him and the smell of him. It's a new smell, an intoxicating smell, maybe jasmine. And she lies there awake, alone in fear for a very long time.

She is not thinking that he will leave her. She's not thinking about Rebecca or what Delia Banks had said or anything like it.

It's more primal, stark and horrifying. This is the recognition that, somehow, someday, no matter what happens, she will turn and find that he is no longer there. And she will find herself alone in the darkness. Again. Just as she had with Jeremiah.

It is about death. And losing Jeremiah. And loving one man.

CHAPTER 9

Alice & David & Rebecca
Summer 1997

"This is Rebecca." She rolled the "r" so it came out RRRRRebecca. "He is here now. He doesn't know what he wants. You must let go of him if he is to thrive. He must learn how to give of himself. He must learn how to love his child."

Alice was stunned at first. The shower was running. She was taking off her clothes. It was night. She didn't know where David was, and he could very well be at Rebecca's. "Leave me alone," she said. "Leave us alone."

"He came to me. I did not come to him," Rebecca said, sounding like a vampire from some Grade B movie. She spoke slowly with her thick German accent. "If he hadn't come to me, it would have been someone else," she said. "Your marriage is over."

Alice hung up then, shaken and wilting, sitting half-naked on the edge of the bed. She began to sift through her memories as one does when trying to figure out the truth. She remembered the weekend that spring when she had the flu, and David took Tobias and left the house. "You need rest," he said, but his tone was patronizing, not comforting. "You just sleep. We'll go."

She hadn't wanted them to leave. She lay there half awake, hot and weak, her breathing slow and wheezy. She felt drugged by the sickness. She heard David call up to the attic, to Tobias. "Get your things together, Toby. We're going hiking," he yelled, and there was a kind of frenzied excitement to his voice. "I don't wanna go, Dad. I'll stay with Mom," Toby had called back. She heard David climbing the stairs and the door slamming and loud voices. Then she thought she heard them both climbing down, all four feet, heavy and fast. "Don't you ever speak to me like that again," David was saying in a half-hushed and angry voice. She must have drifted off for an instant. But she didn't remember either of them coming by her room or bringing her anything or kissing her on the cheek. Just, after the noise, the silence of the house. A few hours later, when she woke up, she went to the window. The car was gone. They had apparently taken the dog, and she was alone. She didn't know whether it was the over-whelming weariness of the illness that overcame her or a sense of sadness and loss, but she wept. She held herself in bed and wept until she slept again.

That night, she awoke to an empty house, sweating with fever, her covers tossed to one side of the bed.

She got up and made her way downstairs in the darkness, flipping on a light in the kitchen. She made herself a cup of chamomile tea, which always reminded her of Peter Rabbit and reading to Toby and Jeremiah when they were still wearing pajamas with little trucks on them and little cloth footies that covered their little feet. They would sit together in Toby's bed, with their backs against the wall and their four covered feet, soiled and sticky from too much wear, lined up in a row just barely reaching to the edge of the bed. They liked the part about the garden best and Peter running like the devil to get away from old Mr. McGregor. Poor old reckless, no-good Peter. "He's the bad one," Toby would tell Jeremiah. Sometimes they would poke each other and giggle, Jeremiah sucking his thumb all the while. Whenever they got sick, she'd give them chamomile tea. They loved the fact that it was real; it wasn't just in some story by Beatrix Potter. That seemed to somehow make the rabbit a bit more real. They would play Peter Rabbit in the afternoons, covering the dining room table with a sheet and climbing into their rabbit hole. They'd beg her to bring them some of that fine, greenish tea in little flowered cups. And Alice would always oblige them. One day, they claimed to have discovered an actual, true-to-life rabbit hole in the backyard, and they spent a good thirty minutes sitting very still at the kitchen window, each with a pair of tiny binoculars, watching that corner of the yard.

This was running through Alice's mind as she steeped the tea in an earthenware mug and sat, like an old rag, at the kitchen table wondering where on earth David and Tobias might be. It must have been an hour or two before they arrived. David was grumpy and went off immediately to his study, without even stopping to ask her how she felt. Toby said they'd gone hiking with Adrian and Rebecca out in Virginia on the Billy Goat Trail. How did she feel, he asked, and was everything okay? She made another cup of tea then and offered some to Toby. "No thanks, Mom," he'd said with unusual politeness as if he didn't want to make her feel any worse than she already felt.

At the time, Alice thought his deference was about her feeling sick. Looking back, she wondered if maybe Tobias had seen something that day, something between David and Rebecca, something that made him feel sorry for Alice or feel some conflict within himself. She had never forgotten the baking of the pies. And she remembered the time, not long after her dinner with Howard and Pam, when they'd all gone to the Thanksgiving Bazaar at school and how, after she came out of the book sale, she'd found David and Rebecca together in the hallway, their heads bent toward one another engaged in the quietest of conversations. She had sensed the energy between the two of them and confronted him again. Rebecca had been reading tarot and telling fortunes that day. She'd raised more money than anyone else for The School's building fund, and David convinced Alice that she'd been reading his palm, that he'd given a donation, and she was telling his fortune and that there was nothing more to it than that.

Nothing, he had said. It is nothing. Nothing, she continued to tell herself, it is nothing. All the fathers seemed drawn to Rebecca. The mysterious widow. Reading tarot cards. Driving that wreck of a pickup. Alice thought she was a loon. She had let all of it pass. But this, this was different, this hike in the woods with the two boys.

"I can't believe you did that," she said later that night to him, after Tobias had gone upstairs. Tobias was only ten at the time and must have been utterly confused that day, she realized later, looking back on it. It was one of those days she would revisit again and again long afterward, when she was trying to put all the pieces of it together—the nights when David would disappear to work on the Houseman project. He would tell her again and again that it wasn't going well and that it was taking far more time than it was worth and that the Housemans, some former ambassador and his P.R. agency wife with whom David was inordinately impressed, were important and demanding clients. The mornings when he would roll out of bed at dawn, leaving her unsatisfied again, and head off to Tisha's to start his day, having hardly slept at all. His face began to look hard and drawn, and, at night, if he did come home, he would drink an entire bottle of wine and unload the contents of an unpleasant workday on her. She would listen quietly and try to be reassuring.

"I can't believe you did that. You left me here, sick as a dog, to tend to myself and went off into the woods with that crazy woman and her son."

"She's not crazy," he said. "And Tobias needs to get out of the city. He needs the wilderness, and I needed time with him." He said it defiantly, without a trace of remorse.

"I don't see at all why you needed company then. And how it all fell into place. I don't get it. And I don't like it."

"Look, I thought you'd want the quiet. And you know how I get," he said. Trapped in a house caring for his sick wife, she thought, like a caged animal. As if that were an excuse for deserting her.

She had been genuinely frightened that day. Frightened of being alone. Of being left. And he had left her.

Now, cradling the phone, she looked down at her thighs, spread on the edge of the bed, white and mottled. And her stomach, beginning to roll into itself in a way she had never noticed before. Her breasts, flattened by age and childbearing and life. What a sight, she thought to herself. She saw Rebecca in her mind's eye, sinewy and dark and tall and thin, and imagined her walking half-naked in her own house and picking up the phone and calling Alice, for no reason other than to destroy her life. None of it made any sense to her. Her own vulnerability and the idea of her husband in that wreck of a house with this weaver with the frizzy red hair. That house with the silkworms crawling in one corner of the kitchen and trash rotting in a little white tub by the sink. She'd been there once to pick up Toby from Adrian's birthday party, not long after the pie-baking incident. All the families had lingered for a time, chattering and laughing and talking warmly to one another. But Alice couldn't do it, couldn't warm up to the place and people. And David didn't want to leave. And now, it seems that The School itself had driven a wedge between them. David had found solace in it. And now, she saw, he had found solace in Rebecca.

That night, after Rebecca's call, when she was certain now for the first time, when all her fears had been confirmed, after she showered and waited until two in the morning for him to come home, reading magazines and doing crossword puzzles and pacing in the night, she screamed and screamed at him. "You said it was nothing," she screamed. And "You lied to me," and then, "You wanted me to send Toby to that woman's house every day after school. What were you thinking?" And she threw a book at his head, confronting him with bleary eyes and scrambled hair.

She saw herself then as a terrible haint of a woman and understood why he had withdrawn from her. She was, she thought, an ugly old thing, used up and worn out and completely incapable now of loving him. She told him that he had to leave the house and that he could never, ever come back.

CHAPTER 10

Jeremiah
1993

Sometimes when things are falling apart, you're not aware that it's happening until it's too late. There are always signs. But it feels safer to look past them. That's how it was with Alice and David. But with Jeremiah, it was different. He spiked a fever one afternoon not long after his fourth birthday. A flu, they thought. But it hadn't been a flu. A few days later, when he had difficulty breathing, Alice took him to the doctor, then rode to the hospital in the ambulance beside him and sat beside the respirator for four days and lay with him in the night. Later, David would insist that they should have taken him to the doctor sooner, that Alice should have taken him. And, once Jeremiah was in the hospital and the specialists started asking questions, pointed questions about their travels, where they had been and what they had done, finally focusing in on the trip to upstate New York, they blamed themselves for not being more mindful or remembering more clearly. But, in fact, it wouldn't have made any difference. There was nothing they could have done, any of them.

And by the time they had all the answers—they being the doctors and the medical establishment and David and Alice—Jeremiah was already gone.

CHAPTER 11

David & Alice & Toby & Jeremiah
Summer 1992

"Ten fingers. Ten toes. One, two, three, four…" She is counting them slowly, Jeremiah's toes. Her hands surround his little feet. It is 1992. It is three months before his death. And this is the memory she will hold on to in the years that follow. These perfect toes. This perfect trip before everything fell apart.

They are sitting on a blanket, all four of them, on a summer evening at the edge of a churchyard on Skaneateles Lake next to a very old fieldstone church set on the lake. She can see it in her mind's eye. There are a few hundred people gathered on the small, open lawn ringed with trees, and it is dusk. At the foot of the park is an old boat ramp made of limestone blocks leading down to the river. She has promised Jeremiah and Tobias that, after the concert, they will all go across the street to the old-fashioned ice cream parlor they spotted along the way.

These are the memories she holds on to so she can get herself through it.

"Look, it's beginning," she tells the children, pointing to the little stage no more than ten yards away. They both leap up, clapping their hands wildly with the rest of the crowd. Then it grows very quiet. "Welcome to the Skaneateles Festival—Chamber Music by the Lake," says an unimposing young man from the little stage.

They had spent the night before in an old motor inn just outside of town, in a single room with two double beds and pint-size bath towels and a grungy tub. David and Alice had made love in the night when they were sure—when Alice was sure—the kids were out cold. Her heart wasn't really in it, only because she so feared waking the children. But David persisted, and Alice knew perfectly well that he liked the thrill of it, the danger, the possibility of waking them. Then they'd slipped out to the concrete patio outside the room overlooking the lake to sip champagne and celebrate. This would be the premier of a new piece, a rather unorthodox piece—not truly a chamber piece, a composition for electric violins and a bass and drum. It had been a coup to get it into the festival and she was excited. They were all excited.

On the way up in the car, she'd tried to hum the melody for them, to get them ready, and tap out the rhythm on the dashboard. David knew it too, from hearing her play it, and he joined in. But he was a bit tone-deaf and always slightly off-key, which threw her off and made them both laugh. Nobody cared. The children bounced about and clapped when they had finished. "Bravo!" cried Toby.

But, after that, the boys grew restless. Toby was chewing a piece of watermelon bubble gum, pulled from a little satchel that they'd packed expressly for the trip. It had infused the car with a sugary cotton-candy smell and Jeremiah wanted a piece. They wrestled over the satchel because Toby insisted the gum was his, and somehow in the fray, the whole stinking hunk of gum had ended up in Jeremiah's hair. Alice was furious and had reprimanded Toby. "Tobias Alan Fisher," she'd said. "You are five years old, and I expect you to take care of your little brother and be gentle with him. And I don't expect you to fight. I expect you to share. Is that clear?" And, when he started to reach over, as if he was going to grab Jeremiah's hair one more time, she'd said, "Hands and feet to yourselves." Stepford words.

Then David had pulled the car over suddenly, jostling everyone, insisting that they clean it up before the gum got all over the car. Alice and Jeremiah climbed out on the side of the road, some dusty road in upstate New York at the edge of a wood, and Alice tried to cut the gum out of Jeremiah's hair using some nail clippers she'd found at the bottom of her purse. By then, Jeremiah had pulled the stuff like taffy, and it was a holy mess. He was kicking and squirming, and she grew flustered and said harshly, "Just stand still, will you?" And he began to cry.

The next day they'd let the kids swim in the motel pool for hours and play at the edge of the surrounding woods, hoping to tire them and then give them a nice long afternoon nap so they'd make it through the evening. Jeremiah was only three, so Alice spent a good bit of time in the pool herself. Afterward, so they could make a picnic, David had run out to pick up white bread and peanut butter and jelly, and chocolate chip cookies—"the big kind from a bakery, not the kind that come in a bag with a picture of elves on it or something," Toby had instructed.

After he left, she lay down with the two of them—Tobias and Jeremiah—and pulled out *The Tale of Squirrel Nutkin*, and before she could even get to the part about Hunca Munca, which was their favorite part just because of the sound of it—Hunca Munca, Hunca Munca, they'd chant over and over—they fell asleep, nestled on either side of her, her arms around them, their heads sliding up against her shoulders. She was too excited to fall asleep herself, but she stayed very still for a good twenty minutes, just lying there against their silky heads, Jeremiah's sticking to her upper arm because of the remnants of the gum. Finally, she disentangled herself gently and got up and then found herself with nothing to do in the empty room. She fussed about for a while and considered turning on the television, but she feared it would wake them. She picked up a Gideon Bible from the bedside table and leafed through it and tossed it aside. Then she just lay for what seemed to be the longest time in the empty bed, waiting for David.

When David returned, they'd roused the boys and all of them put the picnic together on top of the little laminated counter beside the television set, Alice fussing with paper towels and gooey knives and sticky hands. She massaged a fingerful of peanut butter into Jeremiah's hair to loosen up the last of the gum, sitting on the edge of the bed holding him in the crook of her body, and kissing him on the head when she was all done, while David scrubbed the tub so the boys could take a bath. "Your face is pretty," Jeremiah had said, staring up at her. And Toby, resting his hands on her knees, said, very seriously, "I'm sorry, Mom." And she had thanked both of them and reassured them that it wasn't such a big deal—surely she had, she tells herself, recollecting it.

Then they'd made a show of dressing up in their clean summer best—the boys in blue and white striped seersucker shorts and bright white T-shirts and David in a pair of khakis and a crisp, new black polo shirt, and Alice in a soft summer dress. "Ooh-la-la," David said when she emerged from the bathroom. The boys giggled with their hands cupped over their mouths and their heads bunched right up against one another.

If Alice had known that this was going to be the apex of her life, she might have done things a little differently. She might have stayed in bed with her children a while longer, stroking their silky heads while they slept. She might not have made such a fuss over the sticky, gooey mess they'd made of the peanut butter and jelly or gotten quite so flustered over the gum. She might have savored the champagne and given in easily to the lovemaking and spent less energy worrying about whether the boys would wake and hear them, as if that would be the end of the world and enjoyed it that much more. After all, you never know when the last time will be. You never know.

The concert was, David declared, "a smashing success." Toby had recalled the rhythm of Alice's piece and drummed along with almost the entire performance. When she went up on stage to take a bow, the boys had run up behind her and stood at the foot of the stage looking up, their mouths hanging open, Toby holding Jeremiah's hand. She had tears in her eyes when she took her bow.

"Why were you crying, Mom?" Toby would ask afterward, on the way home in the car. She tried to explain the difference between tears of sadness and tears of joy. She told him she was just so proud of all of them and so happy to look down from the stage and see the two of them applauding. And proud of her piece and how much everyone had liked it.

"That's funny," said Tobias. "I thought you were sad."

"Me, too," said Jeremiah.

"No, no, sweeties. Those were tears of happiness," said Alice.

David had reached over across the front seat and squeezed her hand.

That was the trip she would replay in her mind again and again in the years that followed.

To hold on to Jeremiah. To hold on to all four of them.

PART II

CHAPTER 12

David & Alice & Toby

Death just hangs there, the ultimate insult to our humanity. In the year that followed Jeremiah's death, they clung to one another, passing from numbness into private negotiations with God and with the devil and with themselves and each other. Their grief assumed all kinds of shapes and forms and mutated from one day to the next. David immediately took control of the situation, mustering his intellect to give structure to their mourning. "We're going to follow the Jewish model," he announced the day after Jeremiah died, the day that Alice awoke insisting that they go back to the hospital, that there had been some mistake, that he wasn't dead at all, that it had been a cruel trick.

David had held her then, and while she sobbed listlessly in his arms for what seemed like endless hours, Toby looked on dumbstruck, clutching some stuffed toy that he had grabbed from Jeremiah's hospital room in the mayhem of the moment and brought back home. "We're going to sit shiva for a full week after the funeral. We won't leave the house," David insisted, just as he had insisted that they have a bris for each of the boys with a certified mohel—something that was near impossible for them to find at the time because they hadn't yet joined a temple—and a party afterward and the whole bit.

It had been a wise decision, made unilaterally but thoughtfully. It made sense. It would allow them a gradual reentry into the world. It would give them time together to heal. It would help Tobias and connect them to the community that was their temple. That's how David explained it, matter-of-factly, as if it would solve everything. And so, in the week that followed the funeral, after her family had left them with a freezer full of food and a stack of empty casserole dishes and more brownies and fruit pies and chocolate chip cookies than one family could possibly consume in a month, all piled up on the dining room table, they padded around the house and treated each other gently and consoled one another. Alice took to falling asleep in the boys' room, in Toby's bed, comforting him as he drifted off to sleep. And David took to sitting in the living room until well into the night with a bottle of wine.

On the first day following the funeral, Howard came. He said all the right things and spent a good bit of time in Jeremiah and Toby's room, alone with Toby. Alice never knew quite what he said, but when she passed by the room deliberately, lingering outside the door, she heard the words "heaven" and "angels" and something about how Jeremiah would be watching over them now. And she heard Toby say, "Really?" in a voice full of astonishment and disbelief. "Cool," he said.

Pam brought all five of the children over the following day and her husband, and they filled the house with energy and noise, staying into the evening. She brought paella and they told funny stories about Jeremiah that made everybody laugh and cry all together all at once. It was comforting.

Most of the other people who came by that week, business associates of David's and parents from school and neighbors and a few couples from the temple who had very obviously been appointed to the job, hadn't a clue what to say. But they appeared and disappeared with relative ease. Alice cracked once, when Jeremiah's nursery school teacher came by with all his things—cockeyed pictures and pitifully inept scrawlings that represented his first attempts to make the letters A, B and C. She had to leave the room because she couldn't even speak for the trembling of her lips, couldn't make her mouth move for holding back the flood of feelings. She went off to her bedroom and let David take care of things.

Not long afterward, the visitors stopped coming and it was just Alice and David and Tobias together in the house. They were exhausted and distracted. Tobias spent the rest of the week in front of television watching ridiculously inappropriate shows like *Oprah* and *Jerry Springer*. And when Tobias came into the kitchen one morning, where David was trying to concentrate on a cross-word puzzle and Alice was drinking a cup of coffee, just staring into space, and he said in the most innocent voice, "How can a mother not know who is the father of her baby?" Alice very nearly spit her coffee across the table and let out a giggle that snowballed into something she couldn't control, a wild mixture of laughter and tears. Then David started up too, laughing uncontrollably, drawn into the vortex of her hysterics. Finally, Alice got a grip on herself, wiping her eyes with the back of her hand, and turned to Tobias: "What on earth are you watching?" And David got up and turned off the television. It seemed to shake them both out of numbness and into reality, at least for a few days.

David went to work the next day, and Alice took Toby on an outing. They decided that maybe that was enough of sitting shiva.

Then, one night a few weeks after the funeral, David blew. He threw a bottle half-full of red wine against the living room wall, and it hit with a heavy thud, sending bloody streaks of the stuff over the sofa and the bookcases and down the wall. It wasn't the bottle that woke Alice; it was the deep, guttural scream that followed.

She came in from the boys' room and tried to hold him, but he was restless, pacing and cursing. He picked up the bottle at his feet and waved it about, terrifying her. She screamed then: "Stop it. Just stop it. Please." And Toby came in, confused. "What are you doing?" he asked softly, simply. "You're going to break something, Dad." And that diffused it.

In the months that followed, David began to change in subtle ways, ways that anyone would have noticed. But Alice wasn't all there. She didn't see it. She had turned her attention to Toby. She had called a grief counselor for Toby. "He's got to feel some kind of guilt or fear or something," she told the woman. And she sent him in alone and waited in the beige outer office reading *People* magazine. She wanted it taken care of. She wanted him to be okay. She wanted everything to be all right. And she didn't have the strength to do it herself. But Toby, of all of them, seemed the least affected. He didn't want to go. "It's stupid," he said. "She just asks me to draw pictures." He wanted to play with his friends. He wanted to be at school. "I'm in first grade, Mom," he said. "I can't miss school."

Alice spoke with the therapist, who assured her that what Toby needed right now was their love. "Your family and the strength of your love—that's what will heal him over time," she said. "You know, children his age don't really get death. They don't recognize its permanence. He knows what it is, but he doesn't know what it means." She had asked Alice if she herself was okay. And Alice had said, "Not yet."

"And your husband?" the therapist asked.

Alice told her about the wine bottle and the anger.

"Anger's a natural part of the process," the woman said. And she told Alice that some adults draw closer to the people they love, and others pull away. "Sometimes love doesn't feel very safe after you've experienced a loss," she said gently. "It'll heal. It'll just take time. Be patient with yourself. And be patient with your husband. And call me if you have any more concerns about Toby."

Alice nodded numbly, but she never called her again. To Alice, it all sounded like a string of platitudes. A Stepford shrink, that what's she called her in her mind.

As the next summer faded into fall, it seemed to Alice for a time that they might actually get through it, all of them. They had clung to one another for a year. Although they hadn't quite made it through a full week of sitting shiva, they had said kaddish every day for a year. They had marked the anniversary of the death. They had burned the Yahrzeit candle in observation of the anniversary of the day. They had officially completed the mourning cycle. But still it wasn't over.

When, more than a year after Jeremiah's death, Alice began to clean out his things, emptying the dresser and going through the closet methodically, so as not to disturb Toby's belongings, and packing everything up in boxes, secured with heavy rolls of packing tape, she found them unpacked again. Later, she'd discover a book or a boat or a pair of little socks stuffed under Toby's pillow or under his bed. When she talked to David about it, he grew angry. "Put them back. Just put them back. It's not that important. He's obviously not ready," he said brusquely. And when they decided to switch bedrooms, to put Toby in a new room, in the attic room on the second floor, calling him a "big boy" and making sport of it, Toby bristled. He wasn't buying it. When they had moved all his furniture up there and gotten rid of the childish old bedspreads covered with cars and trucks and thought they'd settled him in, he started coming to their bed every night. Climbing in between the two of them. "What the hell is going on?" David would wake with a start, scaring Toby. Alice would scuttle him back upstairs and lie down next to him and stroke his forehead until he fell asleep.

It wasn't until the Thanksgiving of 1994—a full two years after losing Jeremiah—that she looked up from the table at her sister's house and noticed. David had become someone else, someone she barely recognized. When did he get so thin? she wondered. When did his skin turn pale, and his high cheekbones become so pronounced? And where did he get those glasses, little black wire-rims shaped like octagons. Had she ever seen them before?

They were talking about Woody Allen. Woody Allen, for Christ's sake. Someone had suggested they go see his new movie, *Bullets over Broadway,* after dinner. "Not me," said Alice's sister, Catherine. "After what he did, I still can't watch his movies." One of the men at the table balked, and Catherine went on and on about what she called his antics, although she wasn't being terribly explicit, because there were children at the table. She was saying things like "You do know who Soon-Yi Previn is, don't you? You do know what the relationship is? And that's the least of it."

But David, David was saying something about artists living by a different standard and seeing the world differently. "The man's a genius," he said, as Catherine leapt up in a huff to clear away the dishes. Alice changed the subject. "Remember that scene with the nose? Where he took the nose and held it hostage? What was that movie?"

David ignored her. "Take Picasso," he went on. "If you want to think creatively, you have to live creatively. You can't be bound by convention. It's oppressive. It eats away at your soul."

Everyone was eyeing him, dumbfounded.

"What," he said, shrugging it off, not as a question. "You think you can be chewing on a big idea and then give it up just to get home in time for dinner?" Alice looked pissed off. "What," he said again, this time directly to her.

She was upset. But, at the same time, she was intrigued by it. She hadn't heard David talk like this in a very long time. He was getting revved up, defending his right to do whatever the hell he chose. Defending his art. It reminded her of why she loved him —and of what scared her about him.

"So, are you saying what he did is okay?" asked Catherine's husband, trying to reel in the conversation. "Or are you saying, we should just look past it and go to the damn movie?"

"I'm saying what he did is part of who he is—okay, maybe he's a little warped. But it's all part of the same package. That's what makes him so goddamn funny. You want the great movies, you have to tolerate the unconventional behavior."

"Unconventional?" said Catherine, almost under her breath as she swept through the room to clear up another round of plates. "That's putting a rather generous spin on it, don't you think?"

Again, Catherine's husband deftly picked up the ball. "David, aren't you forgetting Flaubert? What did he say, something like, 'Be quiet and regular in your life—and you can be wild and original in your work.'"

"Yeah, maybe that's what he said, but have you ever read

anything about how Flaubert lived?" David replied "He didn't live any kind of quiet and regular life. He was a wild man."

"Flaubert ended up living with his mother. I'd hardly call that wild," said Alice's sister Sarah, the English teacher, who doubtless knew more than anyone else on the subject.

"Screw Flaubert," said Alice.

"Alice," said Catherine sharply, grabbing the turkey platter and dismissing the kids, who very nearly knocked the table over getting up and out of the room.

"I personally like Sondheim's view," Alice went on. She said it because she knew how much David loved Sondheim, loved *Sunday in the Park with George.* It was like a secret code between them, her way of trying to reconnect. "Children and art? Aren't you forgetting? The children? Or is that too conventional?" Alice's remark had been so cryptic, so out of context, that no one knew quite what she was trying to say. Least of all David, who said something like, "Picasso had children," with a levity that seemed out of place.

Thank God, Sarah, who had run off to the study to find some reference book about Flaubert, interrupted the scene by rushing back into the room with the book. Because, not only had David's last comment left Alice speechless, but her remark about the children had made everyone else at the table uncomfortable. In the wake of Jeremiah's death, they'd only just begun to stop walking on eggs with Alice and David.

Sarah passed the book around the table, and they confirmed that, yes, Flaubert had said something about living an orderly life. And he had indeed ended his life in the home of his mother. But when the book landed in front of Catherine's husband, he pored over it for a moment and said: "This is about Flaubert's letters, some review of his work." And he began to read from the review, Catherine leaning over his chair, with her arm resting across his shoulder: "Like a lot of people who have ideas about life, he actually lived another way—and these letters are, in essence, a memoir of that untamed, unruly existence." David looked smug. Then Catherine jumped in. "David, you're gonna love this part." She said it almost scornfully. And her husband started up again, quoting from the review: "'Flaubert believed that this creative bliss—we'd call it being in a 'zone'—was the best pleasure life can provide.' And here's the quote from Flaubert: 'The burden of existence does not weigh on our shoulders when we are composing.'"

"Precisely," David said to Catherine. "That's the point. That's the place where you want to be. That's how I feel when I'm designing."

"I haven't been able to compose like that in a long time," said Alice. "I've all but given it up."

Then Catherine came around the table and put her arms around Alice's shoulders. And David looked up from the table at her, almost sadly. "That's too bad," he said quietly, flatly, just to Alice as if there were no one else there.

It would become a running joke with them, for the next few months. When he started disappearing and hanging out at Tisha's, or when he went off, finally, one day on the back of a motorcycle behind the kid he'd met at an architect's forum, the one who'd come to the door a few weeks before, she'd call him Picasso. "Farewell, my Picasso," she said, smiling. It was her way of holding on to him when she knew she couldn't any longer. She would have called him Woody, but the idea of it was too grotesque.

It stopped being funny, a few months later, when David told Alice it was time to leave the temple. That it just wasn't scholarly enough, intellectual enough, didn't have the study groups he expected from a decent temple. They took Toby out of Sunday school, just like that. And then, within a year, they moved him to The School, the alternative school with the artsy teachers and the knitting classes and Rebecca, the crazy widow. Someone had recommended it to David. On an impulse, on his impulse, they had moved him right in the middle of the school year. More nurturing than a traditional school. That was the argument that convinced Alice. He needs a nurturing place, they agreed, after what he's been through.

But, when Tobias made the move from public to private school, he had to go back to the middle of the second grade; he had to repeat a year. And because they didn't teach reading until third grade, he was quite literally going backward. After a couple of months at The School, the tic started. But David insisted he would adjust, and Alice didn't have the strength to argue with anybody. At one point, they were going to look into it, but they never really followed through. Too much else to deal with.

After they had moved poor Toby out of his bedroom and out of his Sunday school and then out of his real school, and long after they had stopped the therapy, and after David started wearing the octagonal glasses and going to Tisha's for coffee every morning and working all hours of the day and night, he gave Alice a valentine signed Picasso. Tic. Then he became immersed in The School, volunteering all his time for school projects and bringing people around whom Alice didn't know and didn't care to know. Tic. Tic. He started asking questions about Jeremiah's illness and why hadn't she done this or that, asking about the doctor and why she hadn't pursued alternative therapies or taken him to a homeopath or something, as if that would have made a difference. Tic. Tic. Tic. Then, Rebecca appeared, and Alice began to notice the smell of jasmine whenever he was around. He was wearing body oils and using condoms and entering her only from behind. Tic.

It was as if she'd awakened from a daze into a nightmare. She must have asked David maybe a half-dozen times about Rebecca and he'd given her the same answer every time—"It's nothing"— and then her world imploded with the realization that, of course he was sleeping with Rebecca, had been for quite a while, and Alice began to realize that, to all appearances, she was the last one at The School to see it.

Of course, once Rebecca had called the house, ratting on him, rattling Alice, David couldn't deny it anymore. And neither could Alice. She turned on him then, with a fury, stringing one expletive upon another and throwing things across the room, her face twisting in agonized despair and rage and pain, so that the truth of it—and the consequences of it—became irrevocable. "Look," he said, ultimately, maybe in an effort to calm her down or reassure her in some way. "Look, it's not about you." And she couldn't even fathom what that meant. It's not about you. And that was very nearly the end of it.

CHAPTER 13

Madness
1998

This is the part no one wants to hear about, least of all Alice's friends and family, who have heard quite enough, thank you. The part about how David wanted to come back; he really did; swore he did. Two, three, four times. How he kept saying he wanted his family back, but never that he wanted her back, wanted Alice back. About Alice's confusion and contempt and the nightmare of imagining the two of them together—David and Rebecca. And Rebecca, always, in the shadows, sometimes surfacing, never quite going away. And Toby—spending too many hours in the school office because no one could quite get there to pick him up at three o'clock because of lawyers on top of jobs on top of counseling sessions that went nowhere.

In the spring, as the school year drew to a close, Delia Banks had reached out to Alice. "I've been thinking about you," Delia said casually one day as they stood outside the classroom waiting for dismissal. "And about Toby." After they had landed at Delia's house—the two boys playing in the yard, the mothers in the kitchen—Delia had said, "Surely, this doesn't have to be the end of your marriage." And Alice had let her guard down.

"But what he's done," Alice said. "It's so wrong."

"Don't you see?" Delia said. "No one cares anymore."

"What do you mean?"

"Look at Bill Clinton. This Monica Lewinsky business. Everyone knows it's true, but no one cares. It's nothing."

"It doesn't seem like nothing to me," said Alice. "He cheated on his wife. And she was just a child, an intern."

"That little minx. She's a grown woman," said Delia. "And have you seen his poll numbers? No one cares."

"I imagine Hillary cares," Alice had said.

"So Hillary is going to leave him? I don't think so."

Then Delia had moved around the counter and pulled up a chair next to Alice. "Listen to me," she said. "Let me tell you what David told Stephen—what your husband told my husband is that the two of you are getting back together."

Alice just sat there, dumbstruck.

"That's what he wants, isn't it?" Delia persisted.

"I don't know what he wants at this point," Alice said, but what she wanted to say was, "This is none of your business."

"Now listen," Delia said in a patronizing tone. "You'd be a fool to let your own self-righteousness destroy your marriage."

After that, Alice finally decided to take Toby out of The School and put him back in public school, because she could no longer bear the place, couldn't bear to see the brown pickup in the parking lot or Delia or any of the other parents, or the teachers for that matter. Although Alice said it was because she really needed after-school care now and, besides, it must be hard for Toby, everyone knowing their business, Rebecca slipping in and out of the classrooms every day, David wandering after her.

That's when Alice began composing again, working on boorish, gloomy pieces at the piano in an empty house on nights when Toby is sleeping at David's makeshift apartment, grateful that she has tenure because she's so distracted by all of it that she can hardly get through a class. Knowing that she hasn't written anything decent in years. And David coming by to pick up some book or screwdriver or photograph that he says belongs to him, preoccupied, seeming to cave in on himself, losing weight, getting paler and paler, and angrier and angrier—at Alice, at himself, at life. "Bastard," Pam called him.

Anyone can pick up any number of self-help books at the local library to read this part of Alice and David's story, because this is where it becomes hopelessly conventional—despite David's best intentions. Everything spinning out of control. Friends falling away. David and Alice making desperate, feverish love unexpectedly in the daylight and in the deep darkness of the night, two or three times, not nearly enough, when he had come by the house for no reason at all, when Toby wasn't home or was asleep up in his attic. And the two of them arguing about visitation—because that's what they now called the time they spent with Tobias. And money and books and the division of property —which is what they called the contents of their home. And it goes on and on. And even then, it isn't settled.

There are couples who live together for many years. They merge their lives and their property. They have children. But they never marry. It just goes against their grain. Who's to say they don't live happily ever after? David and Alice went through all the motions and all the steps, but they didn't sign the divorce papers. Maybe they couldn't manage the logistics of the thing. Maybe they couldn't face the finality of it. David didn't seem to care enough. "Just another piece of paper," he said. And Alice didn't have any fight left in her.

So they just let it go.

PART III

In the gray light I saw her face,
And it was withered, old, and gray;
The flowers were fading in their place
Were fading with the fading day.

—*Stolen Waters*, Lewis Carroll

CHAPTER 14

Alice & Thomas
2000

"He is a child," Alice says aloud to no one but herself. "I am enamored of a child." Her face is pressed up against the mirror. She is examining the tiny lines that have formed around her mouth and along her cheeks. How close, she is wondering—how close do you have to get before you see them? She sees crevices in her skin that no one else can see. She presses her face a few inches from the glass, but her breath creates a fog that obscures her view.

"Damn." She rubs the mirror with her hands. This is new. This preoccupation with her looks, her face, her age. David has been gone for more than two years. Now it is just Alice and Tobias, and the dog. And now this boy. This boy next door.

"He is a child," she says again. "And you are an idiot." She's still rubbing the mirror.

She met him in the spring, one day in late April when she was working in the garden. It was the same day she discovered the rabbit hole that Tobias and Jeremiah had insisted was out there somewhere so many years before and had watched with such intensity through their little binoculars from the kitchen window. But it hadn't been her garden at the time. It had been David's garden. He had planned it carefully, filling it with the most sophisticated colors and textures—lamb's ears and hostas at the edges, and irises and peonies and lilies in the beds surrounding their brick patio. Clematis climbed the back fences, and ivy grew along the wall of the yellow stucco garage behind the house. It had been charming, really. But the clematis was dead now, choked by the ivy. And the beds were full of weeds. She wasn't at all sure what she could salvage. She had decided that the garden was a metaphor for her life and imagined that if she could just get a grip on the garden, she could get a grip on, well, everything else.

Someone had told her that if you just go through the motions, one step after another, one day after another, you will get your life back. Maybe it was Pam or Howard, or Toby's therapist. She couldn't remember. But she could remember saying, "I will never get my life back." And while she waits for some force to turn things right, some sign, something, anything, she tries one strategy and then another, methodically pressing through the day. In April, it is the garden.

"Hey neighbor," he had called to her over the back fence the day he moved in. He was carrying a crate of record albums and wearing the kind of wrap-around sunglasses Tobias sometimes wore because he wanted to look older, although they always had the opposite effect.

She was listening to the Beastie Boys, preparing for a lecture on black music and white music, and the crossover and the roots of rock 'n' roll for her music 101 class. She had planned it as a distraction for herself and for her students, who were growing restless with spring. She would begin with rap and hip hop and work backward. Research, she would have called it. But he didn't know that. He just heard "You've got to fight for the right to party" screaming from the boombox borrowed from Toby's room.

"Yo," the boy said, as if she hadn't heard him the first time. "What up?"

She was wearing farmer-green jeans and a little tank top and a big, floppy straw hat, and when she stood, she had to shield her face with her gloved hand to see him against the sun. So he probably thought she was a lot younger than forty-seven. She looked younger, but not close-up, and certainly not in direct sunlight.

"You got any roommates?" he asked, pulling off his sunglasses as she stood. She could see him then, his smooth, fair skin and handsome, boyish face. She shook her head.

"We're movin' in today," he said, by way of explanation. "Me and a couple of my buddies."

"You're renting the house?" she said, coming closer, close enough for him to see her more clearly.

"Yes," he said, deferential then, dropping the swagger. "Yes, ma'am." But there was nothing awkward about it. He shifted gears easily, smoothly. "It's nice. Nice neighborhood."

She nodded and smiled and welcomed him, and they exchanged names. Thomas. Alice. And he said, "Glad to meet you," and laughed off a handshake that was impossible, partly because the fence was a tad too high and partly because she had a trowel in her right hand. Acknowledging his own gaff with a disarming smile, he picked up his crate and turned to go.

When he'd gotten about halfway up the stairs to his back porch, he seemed to have a change of heart and turned back to look at her, still standing right where he'd left her watching him, and said rather smartly, "And, hey, you might wanna think about turnin' down that music. Don't want to disturb the neighbors."

Then he was gone. She found herself still frozen right there at the fence for a moment, a bit unstrung. Then she laughed quietly at herself and went back to her gardening.

It didn't occur to her, at the time, that living on top of a handful of young men might change her life. Not then, anyway. But they might as well have shared a backyard for the lack of privacy the little four-foot fence afforded. Their two houses were virtually on top of one another.

Over the next few months, she would get to know two of her new neighbors—Thomas and another fellow, a bit older, named Lawrence. They were graduates of the conservatory. Lawrence played the saxophone. Thomas was a jazz pianist. Their two other roommates were choristers. They all had day jobs and were pursuing their music by night.

The two choristers were pretty scarce, but Thomas made a point of talking to her when they saw each other coming or going, and Lawrence would stop and chat now and then.

One spring night, not long after they moved in, the two— Lawrence and Thomas—arrived at her back door after a ball game, drunk as sailors, wearing Orioles caps with little whirligigs on top of them and red Orioles T-shirts and ridiculously long, baggy shorts, which made them both look round and childlike and silly. Twins, they were, except that Thomas had his ball cap flipped around backward.

"Well, what have we here?" she said, ushering them into her kitchen. "Tweedledee and Tweedledum."

She was wearing her bathrobe, a long, faded terry cloth one and lambswool slippers that made her feel comfortable and look frumpy.

"We are having a debate," announced Thomas. "And we want you to meditate."

"Mediate," said Lawrence.

"I was just kidding," said Thomas. "Mediate."

"Okay," she said in a steady adult voice and sat down at the kitchen table. They'd asked for her advice a couple of times, one or the other of them, about practical things like where to set their thermostat or the best time to put out the recycling. And a few days before, Thomas had knocked on her door barefoot with a pair of shoes in each hand and asked which pair looked best with his outfit. She'd taken it very seriously and made him try both pairs on, and they'd come to a happy agreement on the matter. But this was different.

"Sex," they both said in a single voice, nodding and grinning. "Sex."

"We have a difference of opinion," said Lawrence.

"Yeah. A difference of opinion," echoed Thomas.

"You decide," said Lawrence.

And she said "okay" again, but this time with an edge of skepticism in her voice.

Then, before she had time to imagine what they were up to, Thomas began it. "Sex is about power. Isn't it?"

"No, no, no," said Lawrence. "We've got to set this boy straight." Then he gathered himself up. "Let's see. How can I put this?" And he stopped and thought for a second.

"You don't even know what you're talking about," said Thomas sloppily.

"Play," Lawrence said triumphantly. "Sex is about play."

"Okay, fine," said Thomas. "Power or play? You decide." And he pointed at Alice and then jumped in front of Lawrence. "Me first. It's obviously power. Power over another person. Over other people. If you're sexy, you can have anybody you want. And you can make them do anything you want." And with that he grinned.

"Boy," said Alice. "I'd say that's pretty dehumanizing."

"Exactly," said Lawrence.

"De-what-anizing?" Thomas laughed and then went on. "Look, a girl that's hot. Forget it. She owns you. She's in control. It's all about power."

"You're not convincing her," said Lawrence.

"I don't know why not," said Thomas, who was fairly reeling at this point. "You started it," he said to Alice. And when she looked puzzled, he added, "I mean women started it. Girls started it. Madonna. Britney. They made it a power thing."

"Interesting," said Alice. "I would have thought that men—" But she was interrupted by Lawrence clearing his throat.

"Excuse me, but it's my turn," he said, talking to Alice but then turning to Thomas. "You're just a little confused. Beauty is power. But sex is not about power. It's not about control. On the contrary." He slowed down, as if for dramatic effect. "It's about losing control, about giving up control." He raised his eyebrows then and cocked his head just so. He was not quite as drunk as Thomas and seemed to be chiding him. "Just tell him that I'm right," Lawrence begged Alice. And it was obvious to her for the first time that Lawrence was not only a bit older than Thomas but very nearly of a completely different generation. "It's supposed to be playful. It's supposed to be fun. It's not a competition. It's about flirting and teasing and…well, think about it… remember when you were little—not you, Thomas, but you," he stopped then, turning to Alice. He'd never said her name before, maybe because of her age, and when he stopped, the two of them just stood there looking at her.

"Alice," she said flatly.

"Right. Remember when you were little, running around on

the playground and pushing and teasing the boys. They're pulling your hair. You're running after each other. That's where it starts. You know what I'm talking about. Please," he said, suddenly frustrated or pretending to be. Alice wasn't sure. "For God's sake, just tell him he's clueless."

She was rather charmed by the scene, but she didn't say a word. She didn't know quite what to say, or where it would take them.

"Well, if you don't get it, I can't do anything with you," said Lawrence.

"Do anything?" asked Alice.

"Oh, shit," said Lawrence. "That's not what I meant."

Thomas was laughing, grabbing his sides, his arms folded across his center, all bent over up against the kitchen wall, then pointing at Lawrence, laughing so hard he couldn't get the words out.

"You're a fucking idiot," said Lawrence.

"I'm fucking drunk," he answered.

Then Lawrence apologized and hustled Thomas out the door and they were both gone, baseball caps and all, as suddenly as they had appeared.

In the days and weeks that followed, they both took to sitting on their back porch drinking beer in the evening and calling pleasantries across the fence when she went to take out the garbage or to walk Hobbes through the back alley or to get to her car. The yard became overgrown again because she stopped working in the garden. And she never sat on her own back porch anymore. Sometimes she'd open the back windows and catch the pungent, sweet scent of marijuana drifting into her yard. "Reckless kids," she'd think. And she'd wonder whether they even remembered the things they said that night in her kitchen.

Then one evening, in early May, when she got home with a carload of groceries, Thomas was just arriving at his back gate.

She didn't see him at first. She was smoking, a habit she had taken up a few months before when going through the motions wasn't working for her. "Why don't you try something new. Join a club or something," someone had said. Probably her mother. She'd decided to try smoking, although she wasn't terribly good at it. Before she got out of the car, she took a long, almost exaggerated drag on her cigarette, savoring it and making herself a bit dizzy. Then she stomped it out in the alley and picked it up off the ground to be sure all the fire had gone out of it and threw it in the garbage can behind the garage. Thomas watched at a distance with amusement. And when she came around the back of the Jeep to open her rear liftgate, he snuck up behind her and startled her by whispering "yo" a few inches from her ear just as she was pulling a handful of plastic sacks out of the Jeep. He so surprised her that she dropped all the bags on the gravelly drive.

He was delighted with himself. He clapped his hands and rocked back and forth, laughing with such ferocity that she couldn't help but smile.

"You scared the shit out of me," she said.

"You know, you shouldn't smoke," he said earnestly when he had finally stopped laughing and bent down to pick up the grocery sacks. Then he grabbed a few more from the car and headed for the house. "It's the least I can do," he said, grinning proudly. She followed.

He'd been running and was dressed only in a pair of silky basketball shorts that came almost to his knees and were slung low on his hips. He was drenched in sweat, his hair soaked. She noticed how slight he was then, hairless and slim-waisted. But he had those ripply muscles around his abdomen that you see in infomercials about exercise machines and pictures of sexy young men in Calvin Klein underwear ads. And, as she turned to follow him into the house, she noticed his shoulders and the strength in his upper body, and she wanted to reach out and touch the skin on his back. It looked so smooth and fresh and new.

He dragged all the groceries into the house and set them down on the floor, one by one, then circled around the kitchen as she began unpacking them. She had to maneuver around him as she pulled the bags up to the countertop and flipped open one cabinet and then another. Although he stepped aside whenever she approached, he didn't move away from her. She was awkward, self-conscious, moving with uncommon slowness. And he watched her with an air of composure and confidence. The more uncomfortable she got, the more confident he seemed, until, finally, as she approached the refrigerator with a carton of milk, he opened the door for her, standing so close to her that she could smell him.

"You don't have a husband, do you?" he said.

"How long have you lived here?"

"Since April sixth."

Good God, she thought, he's so literal. "Have you seen a husband?" she asked.

"Well, no. Nobody regular."

"No. There's nobody regular."

Of course, she could have mentioned Richard Cordrey. Just a few months before, they'd made a half-hearted attempt at what he called dating. "Now that I'm dating your mother," he'd said to Toby after they'd been out only twice, "I want to get to know you better."

"He's an oddball," Toby had said later.

Richard had called Alice almost immediately after he and his wife Eileen had split up. "Looks like we're both in the same boat," he'd said and asked her out for dinner that very night. The entire experience couldn't have been less romantic. They'd known each other—and each other's spouses—for years. He was on the Georgetown faculty, a specialist in Medieval music. Gregorian chants, the lute, that sort of thing.

"If there was the least little spark of chemistry, don't you think we would have noticed by now?" she told Pam when, after three weeks, she had decided that enough was enough. "Good God, we shared an office for nearly two years, and we barely spoke to each other."

"But you have so much in common," Pam protested. "And he's such a nice man."

"He's tedious. And broken-hearted. He makes me sad," Alice had told her. And, finally, to put things in perspective, she added, "Frankly, I'd rather spend an evening with you."

Then there was Bill Goldman. Her sister Sarah had set the two of them up just a few weeks before. "You'll like him," she'd said. "He's a poet or something." But he wasn't a poet. He was an editor at some small literary press, and he drank too much, and she found him dusty and gray and humorless. "You're so picky," Sarah told her. But Alice wanted none of it, none of them. They all seemed hopelessly inappropriate, unworthy of intimacy. But she didn't share any of this with Thomas.

"No. There's nobody regular." That was all she said.

"Well, did you used to have a husband?" he asked then. And the question sounded so simple, so childlike that she was taken aback. Here was this striking young man standing half-naked in her kitchen with this body that made sweat form on her upper lip, and he sounded for all the world like a six-year-old. *Did you used to have a husband?*

"Yes. Yes, I used to have a husband," she said, drawing back from him and closing the refrigerator.

He started examining things then. Toby's artwork from

kindergarten and elementary school hung all over the wall beside the back door—bright reds and blues and yellows, people with fat misshapen heads and scrawny bodies. One said *I wish I could fly* in big purple capital letters, and there was a rudimentary picture of a giant bird whose wings were flecks of red and green and gold—only the bird had the head of a boy. She stopped and watched Thomas looking at each picture. She couldn't see his face, only his glossy back.

There were photos all over the refrigerator door, pinned here and there with silly fruit magnets and magnetic ads from realtors and insurance agents. But there was nothing willy-nilly about them; she had chosen each one carefully because it represented a little piece of their life—hers and Tobias's. Thomas turned to them next. The black-and-white photo of Alice and Tobias, holding each other in the snow. It made them both look so small and dark. And there was one of a Christmas party, all the guests gathered around the piano with their mouths open in song; Alice was at the keyboard grinning, a cup of eggnog perched on the edge of the piano. He studied each picture one by one. As he studied them, she studied him, half-puttering about the kitchen, but mostly watching him.

"You play?" he said, looking at the piano shot.

"I teach music," she said. In truth, she hadn't been able to play for years now. It would have required her to tap into a place that was too deep. She couldn't go there. And she had not composed a new piece since Jeremiah became ill.

He saw the photo of Alice and her dear friend Howard, laughing and drinking beer at some Georgetown faculty party. And he saw the one of Pam holding up a champagne glass, but he couldn't have known that was the night Alice and Pam and her husband—the three of them—had celebrated New Year's Eve together in Pam's family room while the kids watched a video, the first new year after David had left. There was a big five by seven color photo of Alice's whole family—her mother, and all three of her sisters with their husbands and children. Alice had taken it on Easter and the girls were wearing little pastel-colored dresses with pretty pleats and tucks and smocking. Tobias stood to one side, awkwardly, the oldest and the only boy, in a navy blazer whose sleeves ended well above his wrists. When that one was taken, David had only been gone a few months and Jeremiah for what seemed like forever. Whenever she looked at the picture, at everyone's faces, she could feel the big void in their souls. Of course, Thomas saw none of this.

He didn't ask any more questions. But she went over and started volunteering information. That's my family, she said. And Howard's one of my best friends. This is Tobias when he was only seven. There was one of Toby and Jeremiah sitting on top of a lifeguard stand at the beach, the sky deep blue behind them. She had shot it from below, so they both looked small and faraway, but the difference between the two of them was striking, even then—Tobias, strong and tan, and Jeremiah, puny and white. That was the way it had always been. It was their last summer with Jeremiah, and she cherished the picture because the two boys were holding hands and happy, oblivious to the dangers that lay ahead. It was the only picture from the past, the real past, their old life. It was the only clear sign of Jeremiah in the room. But the boy didn't ask about Jeremiah. He didn't know. He just moved past it, looking intently at each picture. She didn't say a word.

"Got any beer?" he said after a minute, reaching for the door handle.

"Would you like a beer?" she said, almost formally, making light of his brusqueness, the way a mother would respond to a child who's behaving rudely at the dinner table, part lesson, part reprimand.

"Yes, please. Thank you," he said, without a note of irony in his voice.

She couldn't read him. He seemed to alternate between sexually charged bravado and deferential politeness. Of course, she was an older woman, and it felt as if at any moment he would say "Yes, ma'am" or call her Mrs. Fisher. Or make another cruel wisecrack like the one he made the night he was drunk in his backward baseball cap with the spinning top. And then, a moment later, she feared he would wrap his arm around her and say something like "Man, I could sure use a good fuck." Of course, he never went that far. But, as she came to know him, he would teeter on the edge of such incredible inappropriateness that it either left her slack-jawed or made her laugh almost uncontrollably, part shocked, part nervous, part delighted.

Like the time a few days later when she found him on the front steps of her house. She was going out to get the morning paper and there he was sitting fully dressed in a rumpled man-tailored shirt and khaki pants on her front steps. The shirt, untucked; his hair, uncombed and sticking out all over the place. She was wearing a bathrobe that barely came to her knees and her hair was sticking out as well.

"Hey," he said, looking up at her sleepy-eyed. "I'm locked out. I lost my key somewhere."

She didn't even think to ask him why he was sitting on her doorstep instead of his own or where he had been, and she never even got the damn newspaper but, instead, invited him in.

"Man," he said as he eased into the living room. "I really screwed up last night. I hooked up with this girl. She turned out to be a real skank. Man, I probably contracted about fifty *thousand* diseases."

"I doubt whether there *are* fifty thousand sexually transmitted diseases."

"Who said anything about sex?" He acted offended and then started laughing, rocking his body back and forth in his now-familiar motion, like a four-year-old, completely entertained by his ability to throw things out of whack, to keep her off kilter. Alice laughed too. She didn't even think to be insulted or bothered by any of it, one way or the other. She found him charming, unpredictable. At that point, she wasn't quite sure what to do with him. So she offered him some coffee.

"Don't drink the stuff," he said, as if it were sour mash whiskey. He did that a lot too, spoke in clichés, using phrases that he seemed to imagine adults used, and they'd come out sounding childlike, as if he were imitating something he'd heard on television or remembered his parents saying. He looked around the living room. "You think I could just lie down for a minute. I didn't get a whole lot of sleep last night."

She went to wake Toby and get dressed and make breakfast.

"What's he doing here?" was Toby's logical question.

"He just got here," she explained, as if it somehow made sense. "Locked himself out of his house."

"Why don't you just call them?" Toby asked wisely, his face ticking and twitching at record speed. So she called next door and then sent Thomas home, wondering why she hadn't thought of such a thing herself. Or why Thomas hadn't. But that was some time later, after the grocery day. The grocery day, the day in the kitchen, was the first time she'd ever really seen his body. It was the first time she felt drawn to him.

That day, after she'd unloaded all the groceries and he'd carefully examined all the photos on her refrigerator and he'd drunk half his beer, she reached for one as well and they moved out to the back porch.

"So, what happened?" he said, perching himself on the steps with his legs spread apart and his knees bent, and his elbows set upon them, as if he were the next batter up at the ballpark.

"What happened?" she said, repeating his question.

"Your husband. What happened?"

She wanted to say that he was dead. Or that he'd been gone for years. Or that there never really was a husband. That she'd made it up to protect Toby, manufactured the whole thing.

"My husband had an affair. I asked him to leave a few years ago. It was kind of ugly. Another mother at Tobias's school— have you met Tobias?" That's what she told everybody when they asked. It was her little synopsis, her story, the way she remembered it, as if somehow the fact that it was an affair completely absolved her from any responsibility. She didn't say "We grew apart," which would have made it so much easier for the listener. People sleep in the same bed together every night and drink coffee from the same pot every morning and raise children and share holidays and checkbooks and friends and bathrooms, for Christ's sake, and then, well, they grow apart. Everybody understands that. Or she could have said "We just didn't love each other anymore," which would have done just as well. Or "Just too much loss, couldn't handle it." That would have summed it up nicely. Instead, she went for the drama. The affair. The School. Tobias's involvement. Because to her, those were the facts. So indiscreet, so downright in-your-face—right there at The School. But, of course, she could just as well have spared everyone the details.

"Your kid?" he said. "No. But I see him coming and going. He doesn't do sports, does he?"

"How did you know that?"

"I don't know. Just guessing. He seems kinda like a hacker type."

She looked at him, cocking her head to one side and wrinkling her nose, as if to say, "I don't understand." But he didn't catch it. Didn't respond. So she had to spell it out.

"What's a hacker type?" she said to his blank stare.

"You know. Skaters. Stoners. Hackers. Jocks. A hacker is an abbreviation for someone who hacky sacks. They kick this ball around, from the ankle, you know." He stood up and stepped down to the patio and started hopping on one leg and bending the other one just so, out in front of him as if he were balancing a ball on his ankle. Then he began to jump up and down, kicking fiercely at the air with the suspended leg. "Like this," he said.

He looked silly, dismally disabled, in fact, and then he tripped himself up. It was deliberate, a beautifully executed sight gag. He was trying to catch the imaginary ball that had presumably just flown off his ankle, and he was reaching out to catch it with his right arm and he fell to his hands and knees and started crawling on all fours as if he were looking for where he put the invisible ball. Then he started laughing that uproarious, disarming laugh again, swinging his head back. When he stood up and brushed himself off and sat down again, he looked her seriously in the eye and said, "So, you're divorced."

"Well, almost. Nearly. Soon."

"He a musician too?"

"Architect."

"Really? Seems like he must not be a very smart guy."

"Actually, he's a very smart guy. Just not a very nice one."

He nodded slowly, three or four times looking very somber —like a child at a funeral who knows this is a serious business and puts on a funereal face or a student in a head-on with a professor trying to grasp a complex mathematical formula or at least trying to look as if he's using all his mental power to grasp it. Then he looked down at his feet and up at the sky and took another sip of his beer. And stared off into space for a minute, chugging the last drop of his beer, standing up and stretching his arms in a vast yawn. She had probably taken two sips from her bottle and was just beginning to settle in. But he was already up, bounding toward the back gate like a pup.

"Okay. See ya. Thanks for the beer."

She just sat there by herself and watched him make the short journey from her yard to his, past the lilies and around the withered clematis and past the beds that were now so overgrown, through the alley where they park their cars and through his own back gate, his head bouncing up and down, up and down, up and down. "Hey, don't stay up all night drinkin'," he called over to her when he got to his yard, putting lots of emphasis on the "drinkin'." Then he was gone.

Charming, she thought. She sat there for quite a long time, nurturing her beer all by herself, determined not to be driven back into her house by the simple fact that she was all alone drinking a beer in her backyard. She considered what he had said about Tobias and realized she still had no idea what a hacker was, except that they play with some kind of ball. Sounds like time wasters, like slackers, hacking off. Maybe unpopular kids.

It was getting dusky. The setting sun seemed to dawdle in the heavy, humid sky and then to overheat, spilling out light and color, then dimming, glimmering almost. She sat on her back steps soaking it in. Her mind settled on the boy—all that energy and humor and sexuality, all that heat generated by that compact body. And she felt reassured by it, for no reason that she could put her finger on.

CHAPTER 15

Spring 2000

School is winding down and Alice's dining room table is cluttered with stacks of papers to grade. It absorbs her for now, the grind of getting herself and Toby through the year—convocation, commencement, exams, thesis presentations. One evening, the week before finals were set to begin, Alice was pulling dinner together, which involved little more than chopping a few cloves of garlic and tossing them in a fry pan with a can of clam sauce. But it was late and there was an air of panic in the room. Toby was sitting at the kitchen table wrestling with his algebra, his left eye ticking away like a second hand. There was a large pot of water boiling on the stove, steaming up the windows. Alice turned on the fan above the stovetop to suck up all the hot air, and the sound of it roared through the room, making it impossible to hear, to think. When Thomas banged on the back door, the fan still whirring, interminably loud, Alice was opening a box of spaghetti. Toby leaned back in his chair and threw the door open, and Thomas flew in, breathless, very nearly knocking Toby's seat out from under him, and blurted out, "If we have a party, will you come?" without even saying hello.

Toby just stared at him, righting himself, and Alice, who was about to drop a boxful of spaghetti into the steaming pot, spun around, spilling the lot of it on the floor and launching Thomas into one of his comedy routines, picking up pasta by the hand-fuls and dropping it again, pretending to trip over himself while he searched for the trashcan behind various drawers and doors, scattering dry spaghetti everywhere with a clickety-clack. "Oh shit," he said. Then he rolled his eyes.

Toby was laughing. Alice stood, dumbstruck, and finally said, "Whoa," putting her hands out in front of her. Then "Stop," which came out harsh and loud, because of the roar of the fan. When she switched the thing off, the room grew suddenly quiet and still. "Jesus," she said then softly. And Thomas said, "Sorry about that," looking sheepish. Tobias went and got the broom and swept the pasta into a neat pile and loaded it into the dustpan and into the garbage. And Thomas headed for the door. "You'll come, won't you?" he said, adding "Friday night," before closing the door behind him.

Toby looked skeptical. After Thomas left, Alice pulled out another box of pasta and set their plates down and their napkins, neatly folded at the corners. "That's weird, Mom," Toby said. "He's like twenty or something. Are you gonna go?"

"I don't know," she said, distracted by the idea of it.

When Friday afternoon came around, Alice got a call from Toby at the office. He had been invited for a sleepover and could he go, please, he said. To Will Banks's house. "Adrian's going," he said, as if that made a difference. But that's not what Alice heard. Alice heard "a sleepover at Delia Banks's house" and "with Rebecca's son, Adrian." It threw her off, triggering all kinds of memories. It seemed to her as if every time she tried to put one foot in front of the other, some recollection stopped her in her tracks. And she'd expected Toby to be home Friday night, thinking maybe they would have pizza or something and rent a movie. He would be at David's on Saturday night and all day Sunday, and so she knew she would not see him all weekend. She thought about the boys next door, the party. It had been lingering in her mind all day—Thomas's breathless invitation, the intensity of it and the mayhem that accompanied it. She imagined herself holed up in her own house alone and wondered exactly what she was going to do—all of which had nothing to do with Toby's agenda and everything to do with Alice's. But all this flashed through her mind nonetheless.

"I'm not sure that's such a good idea," she said. "You have exams next week."

"But it's Friday, Mom," he pressed. And she relented.

So on this Friday evening in May, she ended up driving Toby out to Will Banks's house somewhere in Maryland off some back road in what seemed like the deep woods with no streetlights and lots of big, new houses. When they arrived, she waited in the car as Toby walked up to the front door of the Bankses' house and watched Delia Banks open it and poke her head out and smile and wave to Alice as if they were old friends, close friends, as if nothing at all had happened and everything were just hunky-dory.

For two years now, Alice had made a concerted effort to avoid just about everyone associated with The School. And, now, as she made her way back home, she burrowed in, dwelling on it, that last year at The School, stirring up memories of Delia, smug and self-satisfied, reaching out to her over coffee, out of nowhere, suggesting that she wasn't "lovin' her man" and talk of Rebecca and fathers with crushes on her and the nagging question that hung on long afterward: "Is everything okay at your house?"

Memories of David and Rebecca bowing their heads in quiet conversation at the school bazaar as all the other families engaged in their merrymaking, oblivious or maybe not so oblivious; and of the other parents passing around Alice and David's business like a secret. Feelings of shame and humiliation swept through her.

When she got home, she parked out front, hoping to avoid the boys next door, slinking in, wondering if the party was still going to happen, trying to avoid Thomas or Lawrence or any of them. When you live in a city, it is not at all easy to avoid your neighbors. But it is particularly difficult when your dining room windows face one another, as Alice's and Thomas's did. So she pulled the shades and went upstairs and lay down.

Of course, if Alice had been married to David, and the boys next door had invited them to a party, they would either have assumed that it was a token invitation—issued to forestall some complaint about the noise—or a neighborly formality. And they might have gone—together, stopping in to say hello, maybe even staying for a few beers, enjoying the chance to fraternize with new people, young people, musicians, people they might not have encountered otherwise. It would have been an entertainment, an outing, an evening of no real significance. But, for Alice now, it was an invitation of some significance, a foray into the unknown, a symbol of the very fact that, passing forty, she was alone on a Friday night without a husband or a social engagement of any kind or a child to feed or a life. She lay there on her bed, investing the situation with meaning, feeling like a teenager who'd been kicked out of one club and didn't belong in another.

After a good long time, she heard noises in the back alley, and she got up. Looking out her bedroom window, she saw a van flashing its lights and heard the boys unloading kegs of beer. She imagined that maybe Thomas would arrive at her back door, insistent. She wasn't sure whether to hide or to go. She waited for a time and when it didn't happen, when there was no knock, when no one came, as if it would be therapeutic or interesting or just a way to get out of her own head, she changed her mind.

"I'm going to go," she told herself. "And I'm going to be fine. If I'm uncomfortable, I'll just leave." She said the words out loud, checking herself in the mirror, fluffing her hair, turning and checking her left profile and her right and her rear, two or three times before she left the bathroom. All without even asking herself the obvious question: Have I lost my mind?

Alice arrived at their door around ten. She had never been in their house, she realized then, and she had never even met the choristers, although she had nodded at one or the other, now and then, coming or going. One of them answered, a tubby fellow with close-cropped hair and a little goatee. He looked at her as if she were a complete stranger, which, to him, she was. Behind him was a makeshift living room—bare floors, an old square-backed plaid sofa, a flea market coffee table, a Barcalounger, a television and a spinet against the wall.

The room was quiet, with none of the buzz and the easy banter of an adult cocktail party. Instead, there were maybe a dozen young men and women gathered here and there self-consciously—three or four clustered together. Some were so obviously couples that they might have just as well been sewn together. They moved together in unison, sat together in unison, drank together in unison. There was an awkwardness to the scene, a lack of ease. Thomas was in one corner of the living room, drinking a beer, surrounded by three women—all of whom wore extremely tight clothes. He didn't look up and see Alice. He didn't acknowledge Alice. No hello. Nothing. Lawrence was nowhere to be seen.

Alice bypassed Thomas and the girls and wandered through

the kitchen and out into the backyard, where little roman candles lit the walkway from the back fence to the kitchen door. There she settled into a few conversations, most of them centered on what people were going to do with their lives. One young man, an MBA, drew her into a discussion about how the men of his generation wanted commitment and the women didn't—which seemed backward to Alice. She imagined it was some kind of line he used to draw a woman's interest but couldn't think why he was using it on her. There were maybe a dozen people out back, all obviously in their twenties. Mostly, there were young girls and there was no food. Not a chip.

"Anybody seen any food" became her conversation starter. Or she'd ask them whether they were musicians or how they knew Thomas. "So what do you guys do?" she said to one couple. The girl never opened her mouth, but her boyfriend, a fellow named Frank with dark, square-rimmed glasses and a Hawaiian shirt, told her he was in marketing. "Internet software," he said. "We've had a rough year. I'm lucky I've still got a job. You know, with the dot-com crash and all." And when she asked, rather professorially, about the impact on his friends, he went on: "You know, a lot of kids made a whole lot of money in the nineties. Then they lost a whole lot of money or got laid off. You know, it's like we don't really know what we're supposed to do now. Your generation had a cause, right? Vietnam. Woodstock. Right?"

The girl was getting uncomfortable, shifting about, holding on to his arm. She was slight, with sharp features and cool eyes. She wore her hair in a kind of bob and had bangs and hadn't smiled since Alice approached them. She seemed to Alice like the kind of girl who probably spent an inordinate amount of time at the mall and reading teen magazines when she was growing up and wanting more than anything in the world to have a boyfriend.

"Well, not exactly. I'm not quite that old." Alice was trying to be light, but it didn't come out that way.

Then the girl spoke, even and direct. "Well, how old *are* you?" she asked.

Alice was caught so completely by surprise that she didn't know how to respond.

How old are you, anyway? And what are you doing here? And why are you talking so intently to my boyfriend? Alice thought, imagining what was going on in the young woman's head.

All the while, as the conversation began to unfold or rather, didn't unfold, out of one corner of her eye, Alice was watching Thomas, who had by then made an appearance in the yard. For the next hour or so, he was rarely out of view, but he spoke to her only once. "How's it goin', neighbor?" he said. She asked him who the people were and where they came from; and he gave her an overview—some from the conservatory, a few from high school and a lot of friends of friends. He had grown up nearby. "Hope you're havin' a good time," he said. And, when she left shortly thereafter, he thanked her cordially for coming. His last question struck her as odd: "Didya meet anybody?" She said she'd met a couple of people. Then she leaned over and pecked him on the cheek to say goodbye and she could feel him tense up. He got this remote look on his face as if he was, quite consciously, turning himself off.

Then she left. It was a little after eleven, and as she wove her way back to the front door, she saw that in the hour she'd been outside, the house had filled up.

It was the aftermath that got her. By about 2:00 a.m.—and Alice was, by then, out of her jeans, into her nightgown and deep in sleep—the noise started. From her upstairs window, she could see the stragglers—a handful of guys tossing beer cans in the alley and shouting epithets. "You motherfucker" seemed to be the most popular.

Then she heard Thomas's voice coming from the yard, coming from a little heap in the grass to one side of a roman candle. He was lifting his head up, and Alice could see a woman lying beneath him. "Hey, you assholes," he was yelling. "Go make noise somewhere else. I got neighbors." She heard the woman beneath him giggling then and saw her pull him back down. And she could hear them moaning, then, because the motherfuckers screaming in the alley had stopped. She watched from the stillness of the dark in her bedroom, through the screen, and as her eyes grew accustomed to the darkness, she could make out their movements—he had raised himself on his hands and only his hips were moving, and her head was arched back ever so slightly.

She could make out someone else in the yard, another woman, this one on her hands and knees a few yards away, retching. It was violent, raw, unmistakable. Then Alice saw Thomas gather himself up and reach down and tug at his trousers. She imagined he was zipping his pants, but she couldn't really make it out. "Jesus, Chloe," she heard him say. "Jesus fucking Christ." And he staggered over to the poor girl, helping her up. Then he was laughing, that full-body laugh. "You are fucking sick, man," he said. And, with that, the other girl, the one he had just finished with, crawled across to the Chloe-girl and, together, they led her into the house.

All the sounds and activity around them had ceased. The beer cans. The motherfuckers. The other couples, if there were any left, but Alice didn't notice that. Everything was still then. And Alice stood there in the shadows of her bedroom for the longest time, watching all of it, unmoving.

CHAPTER 16

School

Never during her career had Alice been remotely interested in flirtations with her students. In fact, at one point, she'd chaired a committee to establish rules about such things. She was morally outraged by it. David had often kidded her about having "the self-righteous gene." That's what he called it. But it was no secret. She'd lost a close friend, a fellow professor, when he'd taken up with one of his graduate students, the righteousness boiling over.

"It's about power," she'd told him. "The balance of power is off. You're in a position of authority, and it's just plain wrong."

"Look, Alice," he'd told her. "She's an adult. She's twenty-four, for Christ's sake; she's not a kid. She's capable of making her own decisions." Then he'd laughed, as if at some private joke. "Besides, right now, she's the one with all the power."

But Alice hadn't been able to see it. Now, she watches her students with new interest. How do they live their lives? She imagines the fantastical. Are they forever occupied with gangs of friends, like the kids in some Pepsi commercial, out in the woods somewhere in some fictitious place frolicking in some watering hole in inner tubes surrounded by cliffs and waterfalls, all the girls taut and tan, all the boys clean-shaven and handsome? All of them drinking soda from cans and laughing in the sun? All of them screwing in backyards?

But she knows better. She sees the dark, bearded brooding boy in her Music 101 class—Jeff—with the thick midriff and heavy shoes sidling up to a mousy little girl before class, the one who scratches at her head, peeling away flecks of dandruff during all of Alice's lectures. After class they sometimes talk. The mousy girl laughs too loud. These, she thinks, are the outcasts, the smart ones, the quiet ones. The jazz lovers and readers. The boys who play Dungeons & Dragons all through high school, then graduate to the web, preoccupied with Wizards and Warlocks and Witches, looking for false maidens dressed in flowing dresses with enormous breasts and tiny waists or long-legged amazons in leather thongs with exposed midriffs and tight black knee-high boots. These are the kids for whom fantasy has real meaning because they have little else.

Then there are the mainstream kids, she thinks. She watches them too. White kids mostly, from the Midwest and suburban high schools, boys who wear open-collared oxford cloth shirts and jeans, girls who wear bright colored tops and pastels and khaki pants. They raise their hands in class and always want to meet with her about their research topics right at the beginning of the semester. Some of them belong to fraternities and sororities; they go to rock concerts in big stadiums, she thinks, and listen to bands like Dave Matthews and Pearl Jam and they drink too much and experiment with marijuana. They match up in pairs. The girls are possessive, and the boys are nervous about commitment. But they will probably all get married and get decent jobs and have kids.

There are the sophisticated ones, the ones who seem so confident and secure. The ones who were really popular in high school, the ones who had everything. The ones for whom life has always been a little bit easier because they are wanted and admired. She tries to imagine what these, the chosen, are doing, as they make the transition from their high school worlds to adulthood. Are they going to parties every night and laughing with abandon? Are they never lonesome and perennially entertained by one another like the characters in *Friends*? She wants to know, suddenly, about all of them. Whether they're in love and if it's real. Who is sleeping with whom and how often? She wants to know if they know something she doesn't know or have something she doesn't have. She wants to know what they are doing with all that freedom.

Most of these kids she meets are freshmen in Music 101. They're taking music because there's an arts requirement. There's no special interest here. It's a no brainer. So they come to class when they feel like it and sit and listen and get out as fast as they can. They do the minimum of work.

She finds herself watching them more and more in class as the school year winds down. She freezes in the hallway listening to their conversations, trying to remember what it was like to be where they are. To be eighteen or nineteen or twenty-two.

She suspects that they are having sex—lots of it—on a routine basis. She imagines their bodies, lithe and flexible and soft-skinned. She remembers what it was like in the beginning with David, spending entire days in bed, walking around his apartment naked. Everything was an experiment. She imagines that they can have whatever they want whenever they want it. And, instead of being bemused at their hormonally driven lives, their post-adolescent preoccupations, their impatience and impulsiveness, immaturity and innocence, as she was before all this began, back in her old life, she is jealous, and she feels herself shrinking joylessly into herself. She's afraid.

These are feelings that in all her forty-seven years she has never felt—envy and longing. She doesn't know how she will come out the other side of this because she's never been there. The longing, she discovers, is the hardest thing. Not the loss, the longing. The desire for that which is irrevocably out of reach.

In Music 101, she has always tried to inspire her students, to capture their interest before they slip away from her. She incorporates references to popular music, their music, into her lectures. She explores hip hop and rap. This is where she shared her insights on the Beastie Boys. And, afterward, she'd invited one of her students, a DJ, to bring in his turntables and scratch for the class on the last day of the semester. He arrives that day with an astonishing array of record albums, African soul like Fela Kuti and Eric B. and Rakim—old school, he calls them—and classic hip hop like De La Soul. He plays Public Enemy and Run-DMC and L.L. Cool J, just sampling them.

He's a gentle boy, tall and reed thin with lingering acne and close-cropped blond hair. His demeanor presents a striking contrast to the lyrics, some angry and hostile. They're about hate and rape and misogyny. He plays some Beastie Boys and talks about the beginning of a new school of hip hop—more socially conscious, more creative, more obscure, more intellectual, really, he says, turning to Alice. He plays A Tribe Called Quest, Jungle Brothers and something called the Ultramagnetic MCs to illustrate his point. Everybody likes it. And it launches a discussion. After class, she asks him what drew him to hip hop. "It's cool, and alive," he says. "I just always liked the energy when I was a kid." She is touched by him and feels the great gulf between them.

Her blues seminar has always been the most exciting class she teaches. The students are interested in the subject. And they're a broader mix of kids. Some of them are musicians themselves. It's not a gut; it's an advanced class, and they have to put together a presentation at the end of the seminar. She covers everything—Robert Johnson, John Lee Hooker, Muddy Waters, how the blues were born in Memphis and traveled north to Chicago and mutated into rock and roll and R&B. Beale Street and Muscle Shoals and Motown and the Memphis sound. Every semester, the students have heated discussions about their impact on white music and black music, and who stole what from whom and the politics of racism in the music industry. When it's over, they can't listen to the Memphis music without hearing the horns. They can tell the difference between the blues in its various forms, the genuine and the popularized. They watch documentaries in which the subjects' voices are slurred, African-American men and women who were born and raised in one-room shacks on tenant farms in the Mississippi Delta and Arkansas, their nubby hands picking at the guitar strings. Now, this semester, the music strikes a nerve. She tears up when she plays the films and keeps the lights off afterward, to conceal it.

She has loved teaching, thrived on it, but things have changed for her now. She looks different and feels different. She no longer wears her wedding ring. She hears the music differently, sees the students differently. Somewhere in all this is her grief and an anger she can't put away. She cannot divorce herself from those feelings. She cannot play or compose. Now, she feels she cannot teach. She is distracted and disoriented. And the summer stretches out before her like a vast wasteland.

CHAPTER 17

Toby

"Come sit with me," he says. When Alice arrives home the last day of school, she finds Toby in the living room sitting cross-legged on the floor, playing his guitar. He is playing an old John Prine song, made popular in the seventies by Bonnie Raitt. He's not singing, just picking out the tune. He's been playing the guitar since he was nine. They'd given him a cheap, heavy guitar for Christmas that year, an acoustic guitar made of thick wood and painted yellow. It had been an afterthought, something she'd grabbed up at a department store, a shiny yellow guitar with a bright red rim to put under the tree. Something to keep him company. That was the same Christmas that David disappeared with Toby on Christmas Eve, just didn't show up in time for dinner, back when David was still living at home. It was their last Christmas. He left Alice and her mother and her sister Sarah waiting, stirring the oyster stew, drinking too much wine and making light conversation in the kitchen, as if nothing were wrong.

Finally, when Toby and David arrived, Toby explained every-thing. "We had to help Rebecca and Adrian with their tree," he said, matter-of-factly. "You know, they're all alone." But he hadn't said it in front of Alice's family; he'd said it in the back hall after he overheard Alice ask David, in an angry whisper, "Where the hell have you been?" when Alice's mother had gone to put the stew bowls out on the dining room table and Alice's sister was lighting the candles. Alice just lowered her head and shook it, not looking at either one of them, and said, "Jesus," under her breath and told Tobias to go get cleaned up for dinner. And then turned to David and said flatly, "It's Christmas Eve."

For the longest time, whenever Alice saw the yellow guitar, lying on his unmade bed or set up in some corner of his room, all she could think about was what happened that Christmas Eve. About how she'd felt and how casual David had been about the whole thing. Not about Toby and his playing and his genuine love for that ugly duckling of a guitar.

She knew he wrote songs, but he rarely played them for anyone but himself. He'd talked about starting up a garage band. A couple of times, kids from his new school had come by with big, black guitar cases and she'd heard them up there, playing the opening to "Sweet Home Alabama" or "House of the Rising Sun." Once, Rebecca's son, Adrian, and Delia Banks's son, Will, had arrived unexpectedly with Toby. They said they were headed over to David's house to jam, and they'd come to pick up the guitar. Will was older and he was driving them, and it occurred to Alice at the time that Toby had another life of his own over at David's. She'd called David later to see if it was common for Toby, at the age of thirteen, to be driving around in cars with other teenagers. "Don't be so neurotic," he'd told her.

Mostly, though, Toby made music by himself. She'd pass by

the attic door on occasion and hear him, strumming away, struggling to sing. His voice was changing, and it produced an awkward and unpolished sound that she found endearing.

After David left, he'd come by one evening with an extraordinary Martin, delivered to Tobias with much fanfare. Later, when Howard saw it and made a big deal about it, saying "That must have cost hundreds of dollars," examining the fine wood, the workmanship, Alice called it a "guilt gift from David," but not in front of Toby. He is holding it now, his hands moving deftly up and down the frets. The long, slim fingers of his left hand stretching across the neck of the thing, his hair falling almost to his shoulders. He's wearing finger picks and a thumb pick, and the fingers of his right hand are moving with astonishing grace. He plays with a confidence that betrays his thirteen years.

"Let's get Chinese," he says. And he keeps playing.

She heads to the kitchen phone and orders dinner, calling out a couple times, confirming the order with Tobias. "Come sit with me," he says when she returns. She listens to him play, and they sing, old songs, songs they used to sing years before—all four of them and then all three of them—in the car when they went on road trips, songs from the sixties, like "Puff the Magic Dragon" and "Stewball" and "If I Had a Hammer." They laugh when they forget the words. She tries some harmonies, and, afterward, he says, "You notice how much better it sounds without Dad."

"That's not very nice," she says.

He shoots her a look that says *Are you kidding?* but he actually says, "Not nice, but true."

When the food arrives, they spread it all out on the dining room table and make a feast of it. "My fortune always sucks,"

Toby says when the meal is over and she's finished her beer and they've broken open the cookies. Alice's fortune says, "Follow your heart." What on earth does that mean, she wonders. But she reads it aloud, unleashing Toby's imagination. He asks if she thinks she's ever going to get married again and whether she's been seeing anyone.

"Dating anyone, you mean?" she asks.

"Yeah," he says self-consciously.

"I haven't really encountered anyone I want to date," she answers.

"Except Mr. Cordrey," he says. And they both laugh, laugh at the idea of Alice and Richard Cordrey, his presumption that they were getting serious when they weren't, his attempt at intimacy with Toby. But Alice recognizes how mean-spirited it is and corrects herself, corrects them both.

"Oh, come on. You know he's a dork," Toby says. In truth, she appreciates his insight into the absurdity of it. They are a family. They share an understanding of who belongs in it and who doesn't. And they are both still for a time before Toby speaks again.

"I think Dad's going to get married," he says.

Well, I guess we better go ahead and get divorced, she's thinking. But she says, "How do you feel about that?"

"I don't know," he says and hesitates a minute and goes on. "It's like, whenever Rebecca's around, Dad's kind of an asshole." He's thrown his feet up on the long pine table, and his body looks perfectly relaxed, but his face is beginning to twitch, and his eye is blinking like mad. "Like last weekend, he got mad at me. He said I was being rude."

"Rude?"

"Rude to Rebecca."

"Ah," says Alice, digesting it. "Rude to Rebecca." She wants to say the right thing. To say what a mother should say, something like: "Well, were you rude?" She definitely doesn't want to say something angry or bitter like "Well, I hope so." That's what she might have said a year ago, or rather, might have thought. But that's not what she thinks now. "What happened?" she asks.

"They pissed me off. When I woke up on Sunday, everyone was gone."

"Everyone?"

"Yeah. Adrian and Angela and Dad and Rebecca. They were all gone."

Alice has to absorb this. At first, after David moved out, there had been rules, not written rules, but an agreement between David and Alice, that Rebecca would not sleep at David's on nights when Tobias did. And, during that first year, she had made it a point to monitor his compliance—by picking Toby up and dropping him off; by calling David's occasionally; by grilling Toby about it with as much subtlety as she could muster. As Toby grew older and they grew accustomed to the situation—to her presence, to Rebecca's presence—Alice eased up. She was uncomfortable asking Toby about it, just didn't do it. She relied on what she could intuit from bits and pieces of conversations with Toby.

But now it sounds as if Rebecca is bringing the children to sleep at the house. *Of course she is*, Alice thinks. *What else would she do with them? Or maybe they've all moved in.* She bristles at the idea of it.

"*All* gone?" she says.

"Yeah. They all went out for breakfast without me."

"They left you there?"

"Yeah. They should have woken me up, don't you think?" When she nods, he says, "And they came back at like noon, and I hadn't had anything to eat all day. I didn't know where they were or anything." Then he stops for a moment, as if trying to remember exactly what happened, or waiting for some response from Alice. "She called me lazybones. When they got home, I was watching TV, and she called me lazybones. I told her she had no right to call me that. Dad went ballistic."

"I'm sorry to hear that," Alice says softly. "I'm surprised they didn't wake you up."

"And, you know, we're not ever supposed to watch TV when Rebecca's there. I hate her."

"I can understand how you feel," Alice says.

"Of course you can. You hate her too, don't you?"

Alice doesn't want to be in this discussion. What is she supposed to say? That she hates Rebecca too? That she hates David, his own father? And does she? What is she supposed to say? What is she supposed to think? Or feel?

At this point, nothing made any sense to her anymore. In fact, nothing had made any sense to her for a very long time. Surely a mother isn't supposed to lose a child. She's not supposed to find herself trying to guide her other child through this emotional maze. Who was Rebecca to him anyway? His father's lover? What is that? A husband isn't supposed to bring another woman into the family. But he had. Now, there they were—the whole lot of them sharing a life with David and Toby. And what about Alice? No grown woman who's had two children and loved a man and experienced the intimate ups and downs of marriage wants to get all spruced up and go out on dates with the likes of Richard Cordrey and Bill Goldman, like some expectant teenager looking for Mr. Right. It seemed, well, silly. And now, here was Tobias. Dear, sweet, Tobias, ticking and twitching, caught in the middle of this nightmare. There they were, just the two of them, the remnants of their family, hanging onto each other for dear life.

She stopped worrying, then, about saying the right thing. She just said what did make sense to her. "I don't want to hate her, Toby," she said, and the words came out like a long, tired sigh. "But I don't like the fact that they treated you that way. Do you want me to talk to him about it?"

"Nah," he said offhandedly. "It doesn't matter."

CHAPTER 18

Summer 2000

At the start of summer, Alice decides to take up swimming again. For a time, after David left, she had tried long walks. But when she walked the memories would bubble up. Disturbing thoughts, like a recurring recollection of the night not long after David had moved out, when he had come home and said he just needed to be with his family and could he stay for a while. They'd had a dinner, all three of them together, at the kitchen table, just like in the old days, and Tobias had talked about his day. Elated by his father's presence, he'd gone on and on and leapt up from the table to tell a story about his science class.

"You should have seen the girls," he said. "There were dead frogs everywhere and they were like, 'Please don't make me touch those things,' and squealing and Robert goes up to Adele with this frog on the end of his knife." Then he hopped up from the table with the boneless chicken breast on the end of his fork and shook it in his mother's face.

"Good God," Alice had said. "Stop."

"No, Mom, seriously. Adele gets up and pushes the frog back at Robert and it goes right into his face. I'm not kidding." She could still see his excitement in his eyes as he looked at his dad. "He barfed. I mean, he barfed all over the place." Tobias is laughing. And David is smiling, but he has a tear in his eye, and he looks all choked up. Alice is uncomfortable and gets up from the table and goes over to the sink and gets some water.

"Are you okay, Mom?" Tobias starts ticking then. Tic, tic, tic. As if his face were taking a snapshot of that moment, taking it all in. His father's sentimentality, his mother's pulling back, his father's emotions hanging out all over the place. And his mother's withdrawal in a kind of fear. Then he put his chicken back on the plate.

Walking gave her too much time to follow a memory through in her head, recalling, say, how Tobias excused himself after dinner, self-consciously, wanting them to be alone. How Alice left the room for a minute and came back to find David on the phone with Rebecca. He was whispering, although she could not make out the words. She picked up her glass of water and tossed its contents all over him before he even knew she'd come back into the kitchen. And the look on his face: the guilt and grief and anger all bundled together. Then she screamed and Tobias had come down, crushed by the scene. "Get out of my house," she screamed over and over. Finally, Tobias put one arm around her shoulder. She was shaking. "What did he do, Mom?"

"I don't want to talk about it," she'd said. He was only eleven then.

She had to give up walking because the thinking was getting to her. So she decided to take up swimming. She couldn't think in the pool, not about anything but breathing and finding the edge of the pool and the movement of her arms. She was getting it back—the rhythm of it. Every stroke required a conscious effort now, so she could get lost in it. It cleared her mind and made her feel in control of her body. And when her mother or one of her sisters asked her how she was doing, she could say, "I'm swimming," and they all found reassurance in it. She knew that. "Swimming is the new gardening," she tells Pam.

One Sunday early in the summer, Alice arrived home after a swim. She parked in the back alley as always, rushing a bit, knowing that David would be bringing Tobias home at any minute. She didn't want to miss him. The air was muggy hot, but her body felt fresh and exposed, and she'd driven home in only her tank suit, sitting on a wet towel, her goggles still resting on the top of her head. It made her feel adventurous and free, riding around in the car half-naked, cooled by the air against her swimsuit, and the smell of chlorine made her feel young, bringing back memories, fine memories of summers when she and her sisters would arrive home at the end of a long day at the pool, exhausted and relaxed, tangled hair and tank suits and towels jumbled up in the back seat of their mother's red station wagon.

She lingered a minute behind the wheel, listening to the last chords of an old Simon & Garfunkel song playing on the radio. When it ended, she flipped off the radio and opened the door slowly and slid her naked legs out of the car. Thomas had been out running again, and he had come into the alley behind her, but she hadn't seen him. He stopped a few feet from the car, and he watched as one leg and then another slid out of the front seat. She would realize a moment later that he had been watching her. He watched her hop out of the car and slip her forefinger under the nylon that was riding up on her rear, adjusting her suit as she opened the back door. He was watching the small of her back as she leaned over the seat to grab her towel and her bag, sliding it onto her shoulder, up over the strap of her suit. Then, he watched as she turned round again, and his eyes stopped at her nipples. That's when she saw him, just as she was about to shut the back door. Then she stood still and watched as his eyes moved to her eyes.

He wasn't the least bit embarrassed. She closed the door slowly and knew that he was looking at her in a way she'd never seen him look at her before, straight-on, stony, intense. She froze for an instant. Then came the yell, the sound she knew so well, David, calling her from the front of the house, moving toward the back, along the rim of the yard, toward the back drive, the alley. "Alice," he was calling. Sharp and firm. The way you'd call out to a child when you were preparing them for a major reprimand, almost a bark. "Alice. Are you here?" And again, "Alice."

Both their heads turned at once. Thomas and Alice. Then they looked back at one another. By that point, David was in the backyard, almost up against the back fence, the dead clematis. "Where the fuck have you been? We've been here for . . ." But his voice trailed off when he saw Thomas.

"Swimming," she said. "I've been swimming."

Thomas walked over toward his own gate. He was shaking his head, looking down at the ground.

"Well, come on," David said sharply.

"I'll be right there," she said patiently from behind the car, across the fence.

She caught Thomas's eye again as she moved toward him to get around the back of her car, to David, to the fence. But David couldn't see either of them clearly then. The Jeep obscured his view. So he didn't see or hear it when Thomas looked deliberately at Alice from a few feet away and said, almost in a whisper, but clearly, so she could read his lips, "Nice." And then he was gone.

Alice would replay the scene again and again in her mind in the days that followed. And she began to make a conscious effort to look good, knowing that she might see him coming or going, that he might see her. But she is a cautious soul. When she mentioned Thomas to Pam and Howard and to her sister Catherine, she did so without naming names or telling them about the party or the scene she'd witnessed in its aftermath or his leering at her in her swimsuit or about his swagger and silliness. But his age, she did mention his age.

"There's this guy next door and I'm kind of attracted to him," she said gingerly to her sister. "A twenty-five-year-old man."

"Well, that's ridiculous," Catherine said. "Now I'm really worried about you." Howard had laughed out loud with glee and advised her to play it cool. "When an older woman is attracted to a younger man," he said, "the last thing she should be is giddy as a schoolgirl." He'd used those exact words. Then he added: "She loses her advantage, honey."

"It's like an ache. That's the only way I can describe it," she told Pam one night, sitting cross-legged on her living room rug. They had planned to go to a movie. Girl's night out, Pam's husband had called it. Alice rolled her eyes when she heard him over the phone, in the background when she and Pam were trying to pick a movie. But now, sitting in Pam's living room, they are well into a third glass of wine, and they've abandoned the movie idea. And Alice is talking about Thomas. "I'm on fire. All the time," she says. "I feel like a friggin' teenager. It's embarrassing." And Pam comes back with, "Why don't you just sleep with him?"

"I'm not sure I want to go there," Alice says.

"Why on earth not? There's nothing wrong with it. You're an adult."

"Yeah, but he's not," Alice says. "I may be confused, but I'm not stupid. Come on."

"Might be easier than having a relationship with some fifty-year-old man."

"I'm not talking about a relationship here."

"Good. You need to have a little fun, my friend."

"What's that like?" Alice asks. And then Pam says something like "Quit feeling sorry for yourself," and they move out to the kitchen, carrying their wine, and dig through the refrigerator. Leaning up against the kitchen counter, the two of them, noshing on cheese and picking at a bunch of grapes, they keep talking around it, until Pam says: "Tell me about him."

"He's a kid, for Christ's sake," says Alice. "No. Really. Between me and Toby, and these twentysomething boys popping in and out of my house at all hours of the day and night, it's a carnival of hormones. A veritable festival. I'll tell you what it's like. You know those little push toys we had when the kids were little. They'd scoot them around the floor and the little colored gumballs would bounce around inside, making that insane popping noise. Remember those things? That's us. Hormones popping all over the place." Then Alice starts waving her hands around in the air and makes this clacking noise. "Pop. Pop. Pop. Pop. Pop. Pop. Pop."

"Oh dear," says Pam.

But it didn't end there. After her encounter with Thomas in the alley, Alice took to sitting on the patio with the paper or a book or a glass of wine in the evenings when Toby was gone or on Sunday mornings. By July, Thomas was coming by often, a few times a week. Sometimes with Lawrence, his elder counterpart. They'd all sit together on her back steps and talk. Sometimes she'd offer beer. Sometimes they'd bring it. They never stayed very long, at least not at first. It was mostly just light conversation on a Tuesday night or Thursday night or on a

Sunday afternoon—when Toby was at David's and Alice was adrift.

One evening after a round of beers, Lawrence stayed and Thomas left, off to play piano somewhere downtown. He called it a gig as if he were some kind of rock star. "Reggie's playing with me tonight," he told them. "You gotta come hear this guy. He plays a mean saxophone." Alice wanted to go, wanted to hear Thomas play, but Lawrence spoke quickly. "Can't tonight. Sorry, man." And Thomas went off.

"He's really very good, you know," Lawrence said, watching Thomas bound out of the yard. Thomas never really walked; he bounced or lurched, as if there were all these molecules jumping around inside him that he just couldn't control. "He's rather an idiot savant, that one," Lawrence said, grinning.

"Meaning?" said Alice.

"Meaning he's a brilliant performer. You would never imagine it. He seems more like a kid who escaped from *Animal House* or some frat party, don't you think?"

Alice didn't know quite what to say or what to think.

"I'm only just getting to know him," Lawrence went on, as if he was trying to disassociate himself from his housemate somehow. "He's a funny character. He's like a kid."

"I think that's part of his charm," she said.

Then they dropped the subject, but not the conversation. It was a Thursday and Alice had nothing planned. As evening became night, they just kept talking. The fireflies were out and as they watched them twinkle and sparkle around the yard, it took each of them back to their youth. They shared firefly stories—of chasing them down in their respective yards and putting them in jars and tearing off their tails, leaving little iridescent smudges on their fingers. There was nothing particularly special about the stories or the shared experience. Anyone who lived just about anywhere at all in the summertime, city or country, north or south, would have had such experiences as a child. But she was well past forty and he was barely thirty, and somehow the sharing of it gave them a connection.

There were five candlesticks on her kitchen shelf made of pottery and unpolished brass standing in a cluster like decorations from a party long gone by. When it began to get dark and they went inside for another beer, he pulled them out and lit them and turned off the kitchen lights. They sat there quietly and watched the fireflies through the kitchen window in the semi-darkness.

"Did you know," he said, "that the light is the mating call? The males fly around and send out the signal, and the females flicker back at them. And different species emit different signals —like a Morse code."

Alice just listened as he went on. "What's amazing is their entire adult life is the mating season. It only lasts ten days. Before that, they're just little white worms living in the ground. They hatch in the fall and live underground all winter, eating slugs and snails and earthworms."

Alice made a face.

"No really," he said, grinning. "They might spend two or three years living in your backyard in the dirt and you don't even know it. You don't ever see them. They're just grubby little insects. And then"—and he spread his arms out in a big sweeping motion as if he were introducing her to the King of England who was entering her kitchen through the back window. "And then—this!" He stopped and he smiled. "Ten days. That's it. Ten days of flying around and flashing and fucking." He laughed a long, deep laugh. "Imagine if they were sentient, how glorious those ten days would be. They glow and sparkle and screw."

"Ah, yes," she said. "The natural order of things."

"Yeah, chemistry."

"Or procreation, depending on how you look at it."

They talked then about all the things that Alice had mulled over during her youth and over the course of her life. God and whether there is one. Destiny and fate—destiny, they agreed, being those things that you could control, those things in which you still had a modicum of choice; fate being that in which you had none, the inevitable. He believed everything was somehow interconnected. He believed in dreams. And chemistry. "It all boils down to chemistry," he said matter-of-factly. "But I don't mean that in a reductive way. I mean it in a more ethereal way. It's how you make a connection with the rest of the world. That little light on the firefly, it's all chemical. But it lights up the night. Look at them dancing around and look at us, loving it. Chemistry's a good thing."

The conversation made her feel like a girl. She had been so certain, all those many years ago, what she did and didn't believe. She believed that she was meant to be a mother and a wife, that her children were a gift. And she believed there was some force, some energy that drove the universe. It gave life its magic. When she began composing during those early years in New York, she felt it, as an indefinable force moving through her, through her head and through her hands. She would lose herself in it. After her children were born, when she came to know for a fact that people were born with spirits of their very own, it reaffirmed her faith. She knew it because Tobias was Tobias from the very beginning—obstinate, intense, good-natured and full of common sense all at the same time, just as he was today. And Jeremiah, fragile and silly and sensitive and sweet, was so consistently and irreversibly himself. Back then, it had seemed as if there was a natural order to things. And it made her feel safe. She knew too that David was, somehow, her destiny. It was undeniable; they had been drawn to one another by a force beyond their control, beyond her control. Oh, she believed in chemistry all right.

"It's a powerful thing," she said. "But it's gotten me into a lot of trouble."

Lawrence laughed, not understanding at all what she was saying. "I'll bet," he said.

At some point, the point where she found herself mesmerized by the candlelight, and tired and woozy from the beer, he started talking about his fiancée. That's not what he called her though. The girl he was going to marry was what he called her. It was the first she had heard of this girl. She knew that he was telling her because there was some closeness between them, and he wanted to make it clear, without saying so, that this closeness wasn't about romance. He wasn't courting her. That he was taken, that there was already someone in his life. She wasn't the least bit put off by it. In fact, she was grateful to him. She hadn't at all been imagining his interest as a courtship. Somehow, even in the darkness of the candlelit kitchen, she knew that the evening had nothing to do with romance and everything to do with atmosphere. With the pure pleasure of the flickering lights and the companionship and the talk.

They were quiet for a time. The air got a little thicker then. She was resting her head in her hands, her elbows set on the kitchen table, which itself was set right up against the back window. He was leaning back in the kitchen chair, with only two feet on the ground. She bent forward; he bent back. He was smiling and had his hands behind his head, balancing his whole self in his center. His head was thrown back slightly, so that even in the dim light, she could see the edge of his beard, trimmed neatly on a straight line along his chin.

"I knew the first time I saw her that she was the one for me," he said. "There was just no question. But I waited and waited." He stopped and set his chair down on the floor. "It was the most fantastic thing. I wanted everything to be so special between us that I waited more than a month before I kissed her. We had gone out together maybe ten or fifteen times. We were working together. I saw her every day. But I never touched her. Then, when I knew it was time, we kissed."

His smile broadened. "It was the best kiss I've ever had. It was electrifying. I knew it would be like that. And it was. I nearly fainted."

"She's a lucky young woman." Alice meant it. She felt such envy for the girl, for that moment, for his patience and care.

"I know."

Then she told him her story. How she had only ever loved one man. And that they had met when she was only eighteen and that they had separated. And how he had come back to her years later full of promises he didn't keep. And how she had found him impossible to resist. But she didn't tell him about Jeremiah. "We were married for twenty years," she told him. And he said: "Sure beats ten days."

And he kissed her on her forehead and blew out the candles and left her in the darkness.

CHAPTER 19

Thomas

There is a knock at Alice's door. It is Thomas. When she opens it, he swings past her, rushing into the living room. He makes a beeline for the piano, calling back to her. She is still standing at the doorway.

"Listen," he says with urgency. "Listen to this."

She has never heard him play. She listens from the kitchen. It begins very slowly and simply, clear and clean, like a riff from an old Bill Evans number, minimal, stripped of sentimentality. Polished. Three notes, played in sequence three times, then two hands, the right filling in the gaps. She can't make out the song, though. It's unfamiliar and fresh. The timing is impeccable. He doesn't miss a beat. It starts off low, then he picks up the high notes and runs down the keyboard. It is, she knows, just beautiful.

Mesmerized, she walks back into the living room, toward him. He's absorbed in it, and she's watching him.

Then he stops. He plays the opening notes again. "What do

you think?" he asks, looking her straight on, unblinking. It's that forthrightness, that directness that throws her off. She's just staring at him. Like some idiot, she thinks. She's never imagined he would play so finely, this kid from the conservatory who lives next door and preens and poses and carries himself like some frat boy and screws girls in his backyard. It's so crisp, so clean, every note delineated, no unnecessary motions. Smooth.

"I picked it up last week—some of it—the beginning," he explains, his hands set on the keyboard, looking down now. She is watching the shadow that falls across the side of his face, the lines of his cheekbones, the cleft in his chin. He is concentrating; then he stops for a minute and looks at her again, this time offering what he seems to imagine is a more thorough explanation of some kind. "I was listening to Reggie. He's this sax player. He plays every Thursday at the Blue Room." He has told her about Reggie three or four times, but he either doesn't remember or doesn't care or thinks she's forgotten. "He did this number. I don't know what it's from." He plays the three notes again with his left hand." F-sharp. B-flat. C. And again. F-sharp. B-flat. C.

She moves to the edge of the sofa, listening to every note. She is dumbstruck. He plays for ten, maybe fifteen minutes, easy and rhythmic and cool. He has added a new dimension to himself. For a time, she had thought he was all talk, a showman, full of confidence, but she had never imagined that he was gifted. Lawrence had told her.

When he's finished, he flips his whole body around to the other side of the piano bench. He's excited.

"Well. Okay, so what do you think?" He opens his eyes really wide as if to say, "Come on, tell me how great it is. You know it's great." He knows that she knows music.

She speaks softly. "It's really good."

"Yeah, I know," he laughs. He gets up quickly and starts

toward the door. Then stops himself. "Thanks for listening," he says, deferential again. *Thanks for listenin', ma'am.* Then, almost as an aside, "You gotta hear this guy Reggie. He really knows how to blow that thing."

She follows him toward the kitchen, showing him out. But he's moving really fast. "I'd like to hear him sometime," she says.

"Yeah, well he plays every Thursday night. The Blue Room."

"I'd like to go hear him sometime," she says again.

"Well, like I said, he plays every Thursday." He's looking at her now like she's dumb, as if she didn't hear him the first time.

"Well, I was thinking maybe I could go with you."

He looks surprised, as if it never occurred to him. "Sure, anytime," he says offhandedly. And opens the door.

He leaves then. She feels as if she's asked him for a date or something, but he doesn't seem to notice or care. He just breezes on out. Makes no difference to him, she thinks.

CHAPTER 20

Alice & Tobias

By mid-August, the heat is almost unbearable, humid and close. Anyone who can afford to leave the city has left, many for the entire month. Her neighborhood, home to journalists and liberal commentators, pollsters and people who work for politicians and think tanks and the Smithsonian and the local universities, is very nearly deserted. Those who remain stay in. They walk slowly and avoid the burning pavement. The playgrounds are empty. Summer day camps, repositories for the overeducated children of the city's elite—computer camps, language immersion programs, art camps and soccer camps that cost a good deal more than the average American family spends on a month's worth of food—are winding down. The lap lanes at her swimming pool are empty. And there are no lines at the supermarket, no crowds at the neighborhood video store, no school events or cocktail parties or faculty meetings to serve as a distraction.

On a Sunday morning, they rise early so Toby can finish

packing for what has become his annual vacation with his father. She sets a stack of clean clothes on his unmade bed as Toby rustles through his drawers. There is never much light in this room, carved out of the attic, and today is worse than usual. Through the little windows beyond Toby's bed, she sees that the sky is darkening, and heavy winds shake the trees. In a few hours, David will arrive, presumably with Rebecca and Adrian and little Angela in his car, and they will make the trip to the Outer Banks. The summer before when Toby had headed off for this same vacation, she had been angry and called it "a little fake family vacation" when David had called her to set up the trip. Now the anger has gone out of her. Now it is just a resignation and this never-ending flood of memories she cannot control. It's hard to let Toby go but harder knowing who he will be nestling in with.

"You gonna be okay?" she asks. She says it casually, as if it's an afterthought. He mumbles an assent.

"Yeah," he says. "Yeah. Fine. It's a cool place, Mom."

"You're getting along okay with all of them these days?" she asks, trying not to push him too hard, but pushing nonetheless.

"All of them?"

"Rebecca. Adrian. Dad."

"I don't know," he says, rustling through his drawers. "I mean, Adrian's okay. We hang out."

"I guess I mean Rebecca and Dad."

"Mom, Rebecca says the weirdest shit."

"Like?"

"Like, she has this theory that you can switch bad luck with somebody else."

"What does that mean?" Alice asks.

"I don't even know if I can explain it. She says you can take on other people's bad luck. I think she says 'their misfortune' or something like that. When she has a feeling something bad is going to happen to Angela or Adrian—or Dad, she says she'll take it on, so something bad happens to her instead. Like one morning Dad said, 'I have a bad feeling about this meeting' and that night when she came home, she said, 'Your meeting went well, didn't it?' like cheerful and spooky at the same time. And when he said yes, she said, 'I took it on.' She says stuff like that all the time."

He keeps talking. But Alice is caught up in the words "when she came home." She's never heard Toby refer to David's as home; and she's certainly never heard him refer to it as her home, Rebecca's home.

"But, when she gets real weird like that, Dad's always telling her she's crazy. It's funny," he says finally.

"Well, I guess she is a little crazy," Alice says.

"Yeah," Toby says and then, suddenly, as if he's had enough, because she's hovering and he doesn't want it to go any further, he says, "Hey, I could use some breakfast."

She is disappointed. She just wants to sit with him, to be with him, until he leaves. She feels as if she's screwed it up by prodding and prying.

She goes down and makes eggs and bacon and a pile of biscuits. "Geez, Mom. Make a few biscuits, why don't you?" he says when he arrives at the table.

She laughs. "They come from a can, smarty-pants," she says, and they sit in silence while he shovels down his food, barely finishing before they hear David out front laying on his horn.

"Shit," says Toby. He rushes then, barely stopping to give her a quick peck on the cheek. David honks again, and Alice calls out, "Do you have everything?" just before she hears the door slam shut. Toby is gone. She doesn't get up from the table.

She sits there looking out at the rain, which is coming down now in sheets. She should have known, she thinks, should have known to set up something for the day, to have a plan, a distraction. She knows she has to get through the week ahead and the following weekend. To get through Labor Day, when everyone who hasn't left yet will be shuffling off somewhere with someone, families gathering in their yards or trundling off to the beach or the mountains. Ten days, ten days without Toby.

After she's certain that they've driven off, that they are gone, all five of them, Alice takes her tea into the living room, with its windows overlooking the street. It is dark because of the storm. The room itself has an unfinished quality with its bare, wooden floors. At one end is the piano; at the other, the fireplace. In the center facing the fireplace is a Victorian love seat covered in a heavy gold and brown Viennese fabric. It is stiff and formal. The photos and the books give the place warmth, but the furniture itself is hard and unwelcoming—the Victorian sofa, a hardback chair and a wooden rocker all surround a great, big, square pine coffee table that was once a kitchen table until Alice cut the legs off. David had taken all their living room furniture with him, saying, "It's Mies van der Rohe. And it's mine." Her sofa, an old love seat she'd pulled up from the basement and recovered, reminds her of a parlor in which people sat a great distance from one another.

She sets her mug on the coffee table and tries to curl up on the love seat, but it's not made for curling up, so she lies down with her head on the stiff, curved arm of the thing, and then realizes she can't drink her tea lying down. She rearranges herself again and ends up sitting cross-legged as if she's about to begin a yogic meditation. But she's still not comfortable and finds herself on her feet again. She goes back to bed but cannot sleep. She goes downstairs and wanders from one room to the next, examining her face in the bathroom mirror, surveying the TV room where Toby had spent the evening watching movies, drawing the shades in the dining room so the boys next door won't see her, and landing finally in the kitchen.

It is a holy mess—frying pans on the stovetop caked with bacon fat and the dried remnants of scrambled eggs, all those biscuits set ridiculously on a platter at the center of the kitchen table like a prop for an episode of *Little House on the Prairie*. There are greasy paper towels stuck to the countertop, dirty spatulas and the eggshells littering the sink. She starts to clear the table, and when she goes to pick up Toby's plate, she looks down at his napkin, a cloth napkin that she had set so carefully at his place as if the table setting itself somehow made her a good mother or compensated for all her shortcomings, all their shortcomings.

She sees Toby's napkin balled up in the center of his plate, sitting in a wad of jam next to a half-eaten biscuit, and it makes her smile. For as long as she can remember, she has been carefully folding all the napkins neatly on the diagonal after they come out of the washing machine. Those same napkins, blue and ecru with little red hens all over them—a gift from her mother that didn't fit with anything else they owned—were well worn now from years of overuse. And, for all his life, Toby has wadded up his napkin in his lap and wiped his face with it rolled up in his hand like a ball and left it crinkled up on the table in the very same way. She has remarked on it many times. And teased him about it and tried to teach him, on occasion, how to use a napkin and set it just so in his lap.

As he was growing up, she carped on it to the point where David, who didn't like the napkins to begin with, had made fun of her. "Be careful there, Toby. You don't want to crush those poor French hens." Even Jeremiah got the joke, rolling his eyes and tightening up his lips when the subject of napkins came up.

Who would think that the sight of a napkin would keep her from unraveling that morning, but it did. It was a small thing, miniscule in fact. But the familiarity of it, the immutability of it, the damned Toby-ness of it, reassured her and it propelled her forward. So she did what she had known all along that she would have to do while Toby was gone. She made herself another cup of tea and went back to the living room and sat down at the piano.

CHAPTER 21

"How should I begin it?" Alice says to herself, for she hasn't played in earnest since Jeremiah's death. She is thoughtful, deliberate. Ten days stretch out before her, days without Toby, and she is determined now to make something of the time, to dig herself out of this hole. She searches through a stack of sheet music and reaches for Hanon. They are scales of a sort, exercises she has used since her youth to work her fingers and prepare to play. She sits up straight, shakes out her hands and begins with the first exercise. She is methodical. Not as fluid as she'd like, but that will come, she knows. It feels oddly as if her arms are not connecting to her brain. The exercises require no emotions, no real investment of energy, certainly nothing resembling musicality. She plays through a dozen of them and then gets up and goes over to the front window. It is still pouring.

Once, many years before when she was learning a new piece, Alice had asked her teacher: "How do I play it?" It was a simple Sonata by Mozart in the key of C major, and Alice was struggling with it. She had been, always, a fan of Beethoven and of Chopin, of impassioned, dramatic, heavy pieces, using too much pedal in her youth, washing everything out. This was a piece that required a light touch, and clarity, and it was meant as a lesson for her. Her teacher, a Bavarian woman who lived in a small, sparsely furnished apartment in a row house in Philadelphia filled with houseplants and old books and curious little Hummel figurines, had said simply: "Play it as it's written. When a piece is written well, it will play itself. Don't fuzzy it up." And she had walked her through the entire composition—the rests, and the piano-fortes, the crescendos, the phrasing. She played it once through for Alice in the most straightforward way possible while Alice read along and listened.

Afterward, she gave Alice the assignment of studying the sheet music, including all the notations, and when Alice left, her teacher said, "Next week we will talk about interpretation and artistry. This week, you will read it and study it and play it as it is written."

The following week, Alice returned having studied the Sonata carefully. She was fourteen years old, and, at the time, dedicated to all her work. She took this assignment seriously, and it became something of a turning point in her music education. She sat down at the concert grand that very nearly filled her teacher's living room and played it in much the same way that her teacher had played it the week before, without embell-ishment.

"Good," her teacher said. Then Mrs. Bauer sat down at the piano and played the piece again, and when she did, it came alive for Alice. "What's the difference?" her teacher asked. The piece was in four/four time, and Alice could clearly hear that her teacher had put a slightly greater emphasis on the first and third beats of every measure. She was playing in European time, but not in an exaggerated way, just enough to give the sonata greater definition and energy.

With Hanon, her teacher had taught her to play each of the exercises over and over again, but to play them each time a little differently, sometimes with the stress on the first and third beats, sometimes the second and fourth, or to mix it up. The practice gave her greater control and improved her technique.

Alice is no stranger to self-discipline. She plays the exercises, one after another, again and again, each time putting the emphasis on different notes. She is going through the motions. An hour passes quickly, and satisfied with her progress, she gets up from the piano and goes through another set of motions—she showers, makes her bed, does the breakfast dishes and makes herself a cup of tea. Then she goes right back to the piano, plays a few more exercises and looks for another piece to play, something simple, something safe. She settles on the Bach inventions. She practices them as a young student would, working through each one deliberately. And then she stops for lunch, gobbling down a peanut butter and jelly sandwich at the kitchen table, watching the rain.

After lunch, she sits back down, ready to begin the difficult work of engaging her emotions. She picks up a thin volume, Schumann, *Kinderszenen*. Scenes from Childhood. The first piece —played again and again by Judy Davis in *My Brilliant Career*, a film that Alice had loved at the time—is gentle and simple.

After a few bars, as if she had willed it, Alice begins to cry. She knows full well she has not played this piece since Jeremiah died. She knows precisely what she must do, and she keeps playing through it, stopping only when she can't go any further. She is sobbing, fitfully, her hands shaking, her body trembling. She moves to the love seat then and the thinking kicks in. She thinks about Toby's comment, about Rebecca's curious ideas about the transference of misfortune. She rolls it around in her head and sees that it must relate somehow to the death of Rebecca's husband. She remembers the words spoken in her kitchen, the first day she and Rebecca ever spoke. "He died for me. He took my place. Because he knew the children would suffer." If only I could live in Rebecca's magical world, Alice thinks. I would gladly have traded places with Jeremiah. Then there would have been rainbows instead of this half-life. That is how she thinks of it. A life where part of her is missing. Jeremiah, with his long, pale face and puffy lips. She sees him in her imagination and her tears begin to subside. She sees him in the hospital, his rigid body in that enormous bed, his fragile, little white hands lying so still by his side on the white, white sheets, unmoving.

During those last days in the hospital, Alice had invented signs to use so they could communicate. At first, when she knew he could do it, she would ask him to squeeze her hand. "If you want another pillow, squeeze my hand," she'd say. Or she'd say, "My brave, brave boy," squeezing, and he would squeeze back. When he hadn't the strength, she'd get him to blink his eyes. "Jeremiah, baby," she said one night, bending over him, her hands on either side of his narrow body, her face a few inches above his. He opened his eyes. "I'm going to go get a soda. If that's okay, blink your eyes," she said quietly. He just looked at her. She knew he could control his eyelids. He had opened them. He had looked at her straight on. But he didn't move, and his eyelids didn't move. "Can you blink? If you can, do it now." He blinked them and she had kissed him on the forehead. "Okay," she said. "I'll stay here."

She had teared up then and turned away from him. She can see it as if it just now happening. And she sees herself turning back to him and lying down and wrapping her arms around him and holding him, both of them still until darkness seeps into the room and she can feel that he is asleep. She lies there on her side, enveloping him, her body aligned with his. For a moment, she feels the joy of it, of just the two of them, lying there peaceful and calm and together. And she remembers awakening in the middle of the night and knowing he was gone. She could feel it, can feel it now. She didn't have to look at him or touch him. She didn't turn on the light or tell anyone. She just lay back down and slept with him through the night.

Lying awkwardly now on her side on the Victorian sofa, she cups her hands under her head. She moves backward in time. She sees the doctors in their white coats, gathering around them in the hospital room and in sterile, windowless offices with leather chairs, explaining their own confusion. David, angry at them. It isn't making any sense to any of them. *Have you been traveling? Where have you been?* Finally, a specialist from Johns Hopkins puts the pieces together. *A rare virus. Carried by deer. Just discovering the causes. Airborne. You inhale the dust from a dead rodent. Not everyone is affected. Can be deadly.*

The hantavirus, it seems, was just beginning to surface in the United States. The first cases were in the Southwest, but months later, there was another case reported in upstate New York, months after Jeremiah's death. After he was gone. And then they had been over and over it again and again, finally agreeing that it must have been during the Skaneateles trip, must have been when the kids were playing by the woods, out behind the swimming pool. But Toby had been fine. Toby hadn't had a single symptom. So they were never really sure. And they had never blamed each other, not really, not directly or openly. That wouldn't make sense, no. But finally, they had been forced to grapple with the fact that maybe none of it would ever make any sense. And it had toppled them.

She lies there rolling these thoughts around in her head until dusk overtakes the living room. She has spent the entire day, the first day of Toby's vacation, wrestling with her demons. She is trying to accept the facts of her life when a knock comes at the back door. She imagines that if she lies very still, it will go away. But it doesn't. It persists. She thinks that it must be Thomas or maybe Lawrence. But she doesn't answer it. She is in a cocoon of her own making, and she is not ready to emerge.

Lying there, she recalls the days after—neighbors and mothers from Jeremiah's school and Toby's, bringing big casseroles and loaves of freshly baked bread and chocolate cakes in the weeks after Jeremiah's death. When they came knocking, sometimes she wouldn't answer. She would hide somewhere in the house, and they would just set their offerings on the long wooden bench by the front door and silently slip away. When she could bring herself to answer, they'd come in awkwardly and she'd invite them to stay and could she get them anything, she'd say. They'd ask for nothing and sit in the straight-back chairs in the kitchen chatting stiffly about the day-to-day, careful not to dwell on their own children. Alice would just stare at them dumbly, waiting for them to go.

When David left years later, mothers didn't come or call. They didn't sneak up to the house with gifts of food. They stayed away and talked among themselves. Once, she got a call from one of the mothers at The School. "Janice announced in the carpool today that Toby's father is in love with Adrian's mother," said the woman. "What is going on?"

Why, wondered Alice, would anyone make such a call? What could the woman have hoped to gain? Was she trying to tell me something I didn't already know? Alice asked herself. She pored over the woman's face in her mind, a fat, round face, with butter-milk skin and friendly eyes, a harmless face. Alice couldn't imagine what the call was for, except to alert her. Was it meant to be helpful or cruel? Alice had no idea. But she knew, when marriages dissolved, it threw everybody off. The private became terribly public, magnifying the hurt. Acquaintances didn't know exactly what to do. When David left, Alice was in mourning, but no one save her dearest friends sent condolences.

As she drifts into thinking these thoughts, it is as if she is looking for some kind of resolution, answers that she'll never find. Or maybe she's just letting the sadness in, letting it seep over her in the hope that those feelings she still can't shake will vaporize and drift away. She goes over and over these things again and again, thinking, maybe I missed something, maybe if I think and think I will understand it better. She remembers nights when David just didn't come home and sees herself, again, lying in bed wrapping her own arms around herself for comfort, unable to sleep for hours. And how he hemmed and hawed in the morning, sheepish when he came home and explained how he'd fallen asleep at the office again and, no, the phone wasn't working properly, as if this all made sense and everything was perfectly fine. She wonders if she could have stopped it. If she had just held him close and comforted him. If she had just controlled her anger. She blames herself in ways that might not have made sense if she were sharing her thoughts with someone else. David slipped so imperceptibly from mourning over Jeremiah into the affair that Alice couldn't see it at first. Or maybe she just wasn't paying attention.

For three days, she does little but exercise her fingers and her emotions. It is like an intervention, but it is Alice who is intervening with herself. She isn't swimming. She isn't smoking. She is playing the piano. And she is ruminating. That's what she tells Pam when she calls late in the afternoon the day after Toby's departure, after she has showered and made her bed and drunk her tea and spent another morning at the piano. When Pam calls, she is having her lunch and resting from this self-imposed routine—for she has played quite a few pieces that morning. Alice reminds her that Toby has gone off — "to the Outer Banks with David and his crew."

"So, what are you doing with yourself?"

"Playing piano," Alice says.

"Well, that's a good sign."

"And ruminating," Alice says.

"That doesn't sound very healthy."

"No, actually, I think it is healthy," she says.

"You're not smoking, are you?" Good, Pam says, when Alice tells her no. "That'll just give you wrinkles."

"I suspect I'm going to get them anyway," Alice tells her, and they both laugh. "But I think I prefer ruminating."

"I'm going to take you to dinner. You've got to get out of there," Pam tells her.

"No," Alice says. "I'm not ready."

By the fourth day, the rumination has begun to subside, and the piano is taking over. The shades in her dining room are still drawn, but she can't contain the music emanating from her house. And on the fourth night, Thomas is drawn to it. By now her grace and agility are returning. "Like getting back on a bike," she used to tell her piano students after summer break. She has made her way to Beethoven, and the sound of his Appassionata, the third movement, thunderous and exhausting and fraught with emotion, her emotion, is booming from her living room. She is very nearly in a state of rapture. She does not hear Thomas, who has knocked on her front door three or four times in succession and finally settles in on her front steps, listening. When it ends after building to a frenzy, then mutating into something else altogether and coming to a soft landing in the wake of a scramble of arpeggios, an anticlimax of sorts, Thomas knocks again, gently this time, not at all sure that it is over. And she answers.

"Don't let me interrupt you," he says.

"You're joking," she says.

"No seriously, go on."

"I think I've had enough for today."

She leads him into the kitchen, pours herself a glass of wine. "Wine? Beer?" she says.

"Yeah, beer's good."

They sit across from one another at the kitchen table, sipping, staring at each other. "Where's the kid?" he asks, and she tells him Toby is gone for the week.

"Beach, huh. Nice," he says. He looks at her across the table as if he's not sure what to say next. "You miss him?" is what comes out.

"Yeah," she says. "I miss him." Then she tells him it's a good thing, "gives me time to play uninterrupted, to practice."

"I hear ya," he says. "That was pretty amazing."

Then he gets up, shuffles around a bit, sets his unfinished beer down on the table. "Well, I gotta go play myself," he says. "Wanna come?"

But she says, "No, no thank you. I'm kinda worn out."

"Yeah, well…" he says, and as he slips out the back door, he turns back to her. "Hey, how about tomorrow night? I'm playin' with Reggie. He plays the sax. He's something else."

"So I've heard," she says.

By Thursday, Alice is on a high from all the music she has been playing and the feeling that she's regained some sense of control, and the idea that she will spend the evening with a young man listening to his music, a man whom she now perceives as talented, accomplished, maybe even gifted. She leaves the house for the first time since Sunday, since Toby left, and takes a swim in the late afternoon, having practiced through the day and followed her routine with precision.

The pool is surrounded by a deep green lawn and ringed by tall trees that stretch up in a semicircle to a blue sky. When she arrives, save the lifeguards, there is not a soul around. The lap lanes are empty. She guesses that it's because Labor Day weekend is approaching or because it's so infernally hot. And she jumps in without giving it another thought. Her strokes are effortless, and she swims a good three miles before noticing a swell of activity around the building. After a few more laps, curiosity gets the better of her and she stops for a moment at the shallow edge and looks up. She can't see anything clearly through her goggles. She reads a cluster of summer dresses, party frocks with short sleeves and spaghetti straps, in pastel colors and floral prints, fluttering around. They are carrying something, but she cannot make it out —platters, trays, baskets. She watches for a moment, then goes back under, swimming slowly, losing track of time, her goggles strapped tight, a swimmer's cap snug around her head, the rhythm of her own strokes rolling through her mind.

Finally, she surfaces. Lifting her goggles, she sees people all around her, not just women, who she can see clearly now are in their thirties and forties, but men in Bermuda shorts and sunglasses, groups of them standing together drinking beer, and couples mingling with one another. Some of them are watching her.

"Ma'am," she hears, loud and insistent coming from behind her. She turns and looks up to see a large woman in khaki shorts with close-cropped hair and a whistle around her neck standing at the edge of the pool, leaning over slightly so her whistle dangles in the air. And Alice has an unfortunate view up the woman's shorts, so she lowers her head, which makes matters worse. "Ma'am," she says. "Ma'am. You have to get out of the pool. It's six o'clock. We are having an event, a private event." Alice recognizes her as the manager of the pool and realizes that she has been calling out to her for quite some time. Now everyone is looking at Alice, watching as she climbs out of the pool. It is clear that she does not belong. But she is a swimmer. And she straightens up and walks proudly to the dressing room, past the tables lined with food, and the bar and the bartender, and celebrants of who-knows-what without looking anyone in the eye, as if it is her pool and she owns it.

That night, Thomas knocks on the back door at about ten o'clock. By then, Alice had just about given up on him and was on the verge of slipping into some serious ruminating. She'd fought it quite consciously by flipping on the television. And as the evening had progressed, she'd gotten so comfortable with her glass of wine and the idea of not going anywhere that she'd put her head down on the cushy sofa. The television room was the room that Toby and Jeremiah had once shared. When David and Alice had finally taken it apart, moving Toby up to the attic, they had turned it into a nest of a room.

David had hired someone to install shelving around the window that overlooked the backyard, the patio, and they had filled the shelves with books and put in a television with a VCR and a humble stereo system and added a small sofa, a cushy old-fashioned one facing the TV so they could all watch movies together. Then he and Alice found an old pine table at an antique shop in Kensington. They'd set it behind the sofa to provide ample light for reading. When they finished the room, it was a happy household moment, the kind of moment a young couple might share when they've just moved into their first apartment and set up house. Together, she and David had lined the walls with old photographs ordered from the *New York*

Times and old *New Yorker* covers. They'd gone down one Saturday night to his office when Toby had a sleepover and framed them all and then worked late into the night hanging them just so on the walls. Jokingly, they called it their media room and they'd stayed up late into the night, hanging the pictures and drinking champagne in the converted bedroom and finally making love on the cushy sofa with an uncharacteristic tenderness.

This was before The School and before Rebecca, and they were, both of them, still trying to re-create a life together. But, at the time, it had felt just a wee bit forced to Alice, weird even, the determination with which they'd tried to erase the last physical remnant of Jeremiah. Even when they were hatching the plan, ordering the photographs and measuring the walls, and shopping for the sofa and the table, it had felt contrived or somehow unreal.

Yet the room had held up when the marriage didn't. Nestled a few steps from the kitchen, it became a hideaway for whoever needed it to read or listen to music or watch television, or, in Toby's case, as he grew older, to be alone. And tonight Alice had needed it. By the time Thomas arrived at her door for the trip to Adams Morgan to see Reggie play, she had fallen asleep on the sofa with the lights off, the cathode rays from the television shooting out through the back window, giving the room itself an otherworldly feel. It wasn't the knock that woke her but the dog barking frantically.

"You want to follow me in your car," Thomas said when she opened the door. Hobbes was straining at her feet, and she struggled with him a bit at first, pulling on his collar with both her hands, then finally looking up at Thomas as she swung the door open. The piping from a pillow on the sofa had left a stripe running across one side of her face, like a deep gash from her nose to her right ear. But, of course, she couldn't see it, didn't know it was there.

"Hey, what happened to you?" he asked when they were finally facing each other head-on. She had been dreaming again and was groggy and disoriented, didn't know how to answer, didn't even know where to begin. It occurred to her that this boy didn't know anything about her, didn't even know her age, didn't know that Jeremiah had even existed or what it was like to lose a child or to go from being a married person with a family to being something else altogether. He didn't know anything about what had happened to her. He ran his finger across his face, so that Alice did the same and she felt the crevice in her cheek. "Oh," she said, smiling. "I fell asleep."

She sits silently beside him in the car. And, after they arrive at a little place in Adams Morgan, she sits at a small café table up front. The room is dark and crowded. Thomas sits at the piano. A girl in cut-off jeans is shimmying across the top of the bar and dozens of young people are shaking and snapping their fingers and swinging up against one another on the dance floor. Reggie is good, but Thomas is the main attraction. At one point, he jumps up and kicks away the piano bench, slamming the keyboard in a curious combination of jazz and rock 'n' roll, taking old standards and turning them inside out, and rocking the room. Alice downs not one but three bourbons, watching him.

It is easily two in the morning when Thomas brings her back home, and as she says goodnight, sitting in the front seat of his little Honda, she reaches over to kiss him on the cheek, and he turns his head slightly and she brushes his lips and feels the skin on skin and the softness and the sweetness. He's all wound up from playing and the energy of the crowd and the kudos and the fawning young women and the music. And she is woozy from the drinks. "Can I come in?" he asks. And she says, "I'm not sure that's such a good idea." And then it begins in earnest, because, naturally, he is drawn to the pursuit and she to the feeling of his skin against her face. She has seen him in action now, his magnetism, the girls watching him, the whole scene. And, through the alcohol, she is weighing it all in her head when he lays his hand on her leg and there's the ache, full-blown, reaching up through her body.

Before his face touches hers again, as he lurches forward across the gear shift, she presses her hand on his chest and finds her mother-voice and says, "If you come in, you must promise never to ask me again," although she's not at all sure what that means. And then, as his head falls on her neck and he begins to kiss her, she decides that she needs to say one more thing before she's swept up in it. She pulls back. "And you must promise not to make any more of it than it is." And he grins then, because that is, of course, what any young man would want to hear at such a moment.

CHAPTER 22

Alice & Thomas

Thomas stays with Alice one night and then another and then into the week that follows. The sex is playful. There is laughter in her bed, something David would never tolerate because he seemed to imagine the joke was about him, that she was laughing at him. But, with Thomas, this is not a serious business. It is a romp. They talk, but about sex mostly. "You ever done it in a public place?" he asks. He asks her how many partners she's had and whether she likes it better this way or that. She is amused by him and unleashed by him. "Toby comes back on Thursday," she tells him at one point. "Then this will be over." But she says it when they are wrapped around each. "Not that I'm not gonna miss it," she says, which gives it the ring of truth. And he nods and says, "Well, then we better do it again." On Monday morning, Labor Day, having spent the entire weekend holed up with him, she wakes to the sound of his playing Scott Joplin on the piano and he calls up the stairs, "So long, sweetheart" in an Edward G. Robinson kind of voice, a gangster's voice, before he goes. When he leaves, she sleeps, and the dreams come in waves.

She is disoriented when she awakens. It is past eleven. Too much wine, she thinks. Too much lovemaking. She goes into the bathroom and examines her face, pressing it to the mirror. She sees the little crevices forming around her cheeks and at the crease in her forehead. Then she steps back, and they disappear. Her skin looks clean and fresh, maybe from the extra sleep, maybe from the sex. She laughs thinking about it. "He is a child," she says out loud to herself. "I am enamored of a child. And I am an idiot." She says it with a smile. "Ha!" she calls out, throwing her hands in the air. "Ha!" She turns on the shower. Two more days, she thinks. Two more days and Toby will be back, and my life will begin again. Her body feels clean and worn and worked. The impact of his having been inside her again and again lingers, raw and real.

After she showers, she puts on the Bach Cello Suites. Rich and slow and dark, like a wave of chocolate, the music flows through the house and settles around her. She lingers over breakfast, almost meditative, slowed by the sound of it. She wants to compose, to begin a new piece, but she needs to prepare. After breakfast she wanders around the house listening to the quiet, then sits at the piano. She knows she has a small window in which to begin. Thomas will be back tonight. There is joy in that and a sweet, subtle pain, for it is almost over. She throws these two conflicting emotions around in her head. She jots down some notes, but she does not play.

On Tuesday night he comes late. They make love in her bed with the lights on. Afterward, he lies on his side resting on his elbow, his head in his hand. She is lying flat on her back, looking up at the ceiling. He runs his fingers along her cheek and her neck. He calls her well preserved. "Oh, that's nice," she says.

"No, I mean it," he says. She laughs. She has the covers pulled up around her breasts, but he draws them down and runs his fingers across her chest and toward her stomach. He is watching his own hand move across her flesh. This is a new intimacy, outside of the realm of the sex itself. He is examining her, exploring her and watching his own hand intently as it moves across her body. There is a shyness to her. With some deliberateness, she has not paraded around naked in front of him, on display. She has been discreet about her own body, for she is not in her twenties. But he persists, gently, avoiding her eyes, pushing the covers down further, slowly, across her hips. He touches the stretch marks on either side of her belly. "These are from having a baby, aren't they?" She tugs the covers back up and turns to face him. "Babies, you mean."

"Babies," he says flatly. It's not a question.

"Two babies," she says.

"Two babies," he says, as if that's okay with him. And then, without any prompting, she tells him about Jeremiah, about the illness, about his death.

"How old was he?" Thomas asks.

"Four," she says. She is resting on her elbow now, facing him, head-on. They are not touching. She has tears in her eyes. He can see them.

"What about Toby?"

"He didn't contract it, for some reason," she says. "He was fine."

"No. I mean how old was Toby?"

"Six," she says.

He lies down on the pillow, puts his hands behind his head, looks up at the ceiling, lying still for a time. "I gotta brother," he says. She is lying down now too, facing him, her hands pressed together beneath her cheek. "Bummer," he says, unmoving. She turns off the light then, and, after a time, he turns over and holds her through the night. But she cannot feel his flesh, just his arms around her and the sheets snug between them. She is over-whelmed by a sense of relief, of peace.

The next morning, she must go to school, to a faculty meeting to kick off the fall semester. She puts on a little slip of a dress, revealing her arms, tan and taut, strengthened by the swimming. People tell her she looks radiant. "Why you're glow-ing," says Howard. Then, guessing, imagining what has hap-pened, he laughs. "Oh my God, you didn't? You did, didn't you? Oh my God." She is out of character now. She feels elevated in some way, mellowed. Who would ever imagine Alice doing such a thing? She feels as if Oprah might jump into the scene and say, "You go girl." It makes her smile.

When she arrives home that evening, Alice heads for the kitchen and uncorks a bottle of Pinot Grigio. She sets the glass down on the kitchen table and raises her arms in an exaggerated stretch high in the air, unwinding, her fingertips reaching up the ceiling, her hem rising to her thighs. Then, leaning with one hand against a kitchen chair, she slips off her heels one at a time. That's when she sees Thomas, standing there watching her through the kitchen window.

She'd been half expecting him but wasn't at all sure when he'd come or what to expect. She's quiet, reserved. He seems not to notice. He is wearing a T-shirt that exaggerates the breadth of his upper body and a pair of faded jeans. His hair is akimbo, the cowlick shooting a few strands haphazardly across one eyebrow, but they are shiny, and she sees that he has carefully arranged them there with hair gel. He looks freshly showered and smells like Irish Spring and baby powder, and his face is flushed. The casualness, even recklessness, of the past few days are gone. She feels more like herself than she has in a long time. And she senses the weight of the moment. Their last night. He is all cleaned up and it makes her feel awkward. She is ready to let it go, but not at all sure how he will handle it. She thinks he is about to make a speech or embrace her and deliver some heartfelt farewell or, worse still, condolences.

But he lurches past her. "I got somethin' for ya'," he says, agitated, waving a CD case in the air. His face full of expectation and excitement and energy, he grins and raises his eyebrows. "It's mine. I want to play it for you."

So she follows him into her living room and watches him bend down and put the disk in the player, following the curve of his back and the shape of his frame with her eyes as he moves, taking it all in. She curls up on one end of the little Victorian sofa with her wine. "It's for you," he says.

As it begins, he walks in circles around the odd collection of living room furniture for a time, his hands in his pockets. He is jumpy. The music starts with a saxophone, then a light brush of a drumbeat, then Thomas comes in on the piano. She sits very still, listening intently. He settles in on the piano bench behind her, facing her back. It is his piece, she realizes, something he has written. Occasionally, she speaks. "That's nice," she says. Or "Who decided to add the bass there?" And he answers something about the producer or how he wanted to build to a kind of crescendo here or there, or that Bob, the bassist, just threw that in and it works. They are all about the music.

She turns to him when she speaks, then turns back to the CD player, as if she has to be facing it, as if she is watching it instead of listening to it. At one point, she turns to look at him, expecting him to be watching her from behind, but he is bent over on the piano bench, his elbows on his knees, his head down, his hands clasped together against his forehead, listening, breathing heavily.

The first piece is soft and smooth and slow and lasts about ten minutes. The second is longer, more complex. It's a fusion of hip-hop and jazz, much like what she had heard him play in Adams Morgan. It has kind of a funky seventies feel to it, and the beat picks up considerably. Awakened by it, she turns gleefully to him, grinning broadly at the first few measures. "I love this one," she says, recognizing it. It lifts her. He throws his head back in a deep laugh and hops up from the piano bench and grabs her then by the hand, drawing her close to him and dancing the jitterbug, swinging her to one side and then another.

They are facing each other, his hands on her hips, resting on her silky dress, still half-swaying when it stops. She is out of breath. He isn't. Neither of them seems able or willing to let the stillness settle around them. "You're a good dancer," he says finally, sounding like a child delivering the purest of compliments. "You ever hear that poem—the one that goes, 'Love like you've never been hurt. Dance like nobody's watching?' I like that line. 'Dance like nobody's watching.' You ever notice how most people don't know how to dance that way?"

"No." She is amused. *Love like you've never been hurt.* "No, I've never heard that poem." It sounds more like a greeting card to her anyway.

"But you know how," he says. Then he jolts away from her and starts it up a second time. He has a devilish look in his eyes, dancing toward her from across the room, taking giant steps and flapping his elbows against his rib cage, making his way around the Victorian sofa one leap at a time. He is making a game of it. She laughs a hearty, grown-up laugh and sweeps toward him, taking hold of his hand, moving with abandon, first in a circle around him, then swinging in close. Her hand around his neck, his arm across her back, they bob up and down together, their faces relaxing with pleasure, the music taking hold of them both and swinging them in its arms. It goes on and on, and she is grounded in it.

This time, when the music stops, Thomas bows a deep, gracious bow and then circles around her and plops down on the old Victorian sofa so hard she thinks the springs will break. He looks ridiculously out of place. The coffee table stands between them.

"Well?" he says, expectantly, holding up the thin, plastic CD case and swiveling it in the air. He seems nervous now.

"I love it," she says. "It's brilliant, really. Beautiful."

"Brilliant?" he says with an enthusiasm so fresh it is disarming. "Really?" He hesitates, then adds, "But do you think it's original?"

"It's better than original. It's good," she says, firmly, authoritatively.

He jumps up from the sofa. "Yes!" he says, pumping a fist in the air, like a quarterback who just scored a touchdown. Then he reaches over the coffee table, his knees bumping up against the thing, and slaps her five. It catches her off guard, and she barely gets her hand in the air in time. He laughs.

"Hey, thank you," he says, more serious now, and turns awkwardly, sidling out from behind the coffee table and walking over to the CD player. "Really," he adds, with a note of sincerity. He ejects the CD and puts it in the case and hands it to her. They are standing a few feet from one another. She looks intently at the blank cover. There's nothing on it. No picture. No writing.

"It's just a demo. But you can keep it if you want," he says. And then he backs away from her and around the loveseat to the front door with such speed that she hasn't time to react and, halfway out, he turns back to her and says, "Take care of yourself."

She's startled and calls out, "Bye," crisply, almost as an

afterthought. And, although she'd expected him to stay, imagined at first that the dancing was foreplay, she soon recognizes that it is something else, something sweeter. She rolls it around in her head. And she's okay with it, fine with it, in fact.

That night, after dinner, she will listen to Thomas's CD again and again. In the morning she'll load it into the CD player in her car and play it over and over on her way to pick up Toby when he returns, on trips to the supermarket and, ultimately, back to school and everywhere in between, parsing the first piece, the minimal jazzy one, and indulging in the second, the rhythmic dance number, again and again, drawing energy from it and ideas.

CHAPTER 23

Alice

In the weeks that follow, after Toby returns and on evenings when he is at David's and into the night, she will sit at her grand piano for hours with a glass of wine or, sometimes, nothing at all, in a kind of a trance, making notations now and then in a thick spiral notebook and working through ideas that keep bubbling up in her head.

Alice is composing. And, for Alice, composition is a tricky business. It starts not with a melody but with an idea. Alice has to have a hook around which an entire piece is built, an idea, a concept. David taught her that. Years ago, when she was pregnant with Toby, six months into it, composing the piece that she hoped would win her tenure and flummoxed by her pregnancy, she'd turned to David for help. "What's your idea?" he'd asked her. And they'd talked quite a bit about how he approached his architecture and how she might approach her music. Afterward, she'd written a stunning piece. It was in nine parts, not only mirroring the stages she was going through in her pregnancy and the maelstrom of conflicting emotions she was experiencing—feelings of dread, anticipation, helplessness and joy—but also the stages this tiny being, swelling up inside her belly, was going through. The music gave her feelings a voice; the idea gave the piece its structure.

Now the idea that's beginning to gel in her head and find its way to her fingers centers on Thomas—not just what Thomas has written, not just his music, not even Thomas himself. For, even now, she knows almost nothing of him. But she is composing around the idea of who Thomas is in relation to her, his many faces as seen through the prism of her perceptions. Man-boy. Part genius, part jester, part lover, part child. The ideas linger in the back of her mind each day and find expression in the evenings, flowing out of her through the piano and onto the page.

She weaves the themes she hears on his CD through her work, transposing them, transforming them. She gives voice to his curious self—his boyishness, his carelessness, his guilelessness, his humor and, in the end, his wisdom. She sets his youth and sexuality against her age, her experience, her fragility and fears. She is completely absorbed in it. It will sound unlike anything she's ever written before. The piece that emerges is rich and complex.

Thomas, it seems, has become her muse.

PART IV

CHAPTER 24

Fall 2000

In reality, there are no clear endings or beginnings, except birth and death, and the day you choose to take someone on for life. And once you do, letting go if you have to is like tugging at taffy or trying to get gum out of your hair, sticky and maddening and messy, requiring enormous patience, and impossible until it's done. If it goes on too long, it makes you crazy. Or maybe it makes you crazy anyway, at least for a time. Anyone who says otherwise isn't telling the truth. Even if you've fallen in love already or jumped into bed with someone else, you're still in for a little madness. And that madness touches everyone in its path.

In the fall of 2000, Alice is back at the university, engaged by her work, teaching and composing, and as the season unfolds, a feeling of well being kicks in, as if the worst might well be over. In the weeks following Toby's visit to the Outer Banks and Alice's interlude with Thomas, the boys next door had shifted their attention away from Alice and toward Toby, befriending him in a protective, older brother kind of way. And, perhaps as a consequence, Toby, too, seems more comfortable in his skin, more at ease, less, well, ticky.

But come November, all hell breaks loose. David is out of town for more than a week, gone to Chicago to participate in a charette, something to do with Wrigley Field and the surrounding neighborhood. Toby is home with Alice for a good long stretch. In the wake of the presidential election, pretty much everyone they know is preoccupied with the results, the Florida recount and what will happen next. The Friday after Election Day, Alice joins her colleagues at the Celtic Tavern in Georgetown to vent, to talk politics and to scratch their collective heads in wonderment. Howard is insanely angry at the Nader contingent. "Sometimes you have to vote your conscience," Alice says, in their defense and in her own. And someone from the political science department talks about the two-party system and how the Republicans and Democrats are basically the same—"They're all in the pockets of the big corporations. It's just not working for the American people." There is much speculation about what will happen to the Supreme Court if Bush gets into office. "I suspect we're going to lose some freedoms," Howard says. "You ladies are going to lose some freedoms." The women at the table start booing loudly, at Howard and the word "ladies" and at the idea of the Supreme Court and George Bush whittling away their rights. In the end, Alice imbibes so much bourbon that Howard has to give her a ride home.

By the time she gets there, it's dark, close to seven and she's still feeling the effects of the whisky. Howard insists on walking her to the door and Thomas greets them both. Toby and Thomas have apparently been playing video games, which is not uncommon these days. Howard's rapid departure triggers a remark from Thomas about who exactly that old man is. So Alice takes him by the elbow and leads him to the refrigerator, pointing out Howard's photograph.

"My friend Howard," she says.

"Just lookin' out for ya," he replies.

Then Toby surfaces. He wants to know if he can go to a party at Will Banks's house, a Halloween party—or something akin to a Halloween party.

"Tonight?" says Alice.

"Yeah," says Thomas. "And where's your costume?"

"Well, it's not exactly for Halloween," Toby says, then to his mother, "You remember, Samhain," he drags the words out, rolling his eyes. "You know, the Celtic New Year, the ritual celebration of the end of the fall harvest."

"Cool," Thomas says, grinning. "You gotta bring a gourd or something?"

Toby is embarrassed, and a bit of a tic kicks in, but it's hardly noticeable. "There'll be parents there," he says earnestly, turning to Alice. And, at first, she thinks he is reassuring her that the party will be chaperoned, as any teenager might do. But, instead, in his own way, he is telling her that the party is for families from The School, and he knows full well his mother won't want to be among them, wouldn't choose to be, wouldn't be invited. "Can you just drop me off?" he asks. "I can spend the night. Or get a ride home or something." But Alice doesn't have a car. She has left it in Georgetown. So Thomas volunteers to drive Toby to Will Banks's house. And, perhaps inspired by the alcohol, Alice says she'll come along for the ride.

She is casual about the whole thing, too casual, she would think later. For when they arrive, she sees a dozen cars parked out front, and as they make their way around the long, circular drive and out toward the street, she sees Rebecca getting out of her big, brown truck at the foot of the drive. Their headlights shine on the frizzy hair blowing in the wind and through Rebecca's flimsy skirt, revealing the curves of her body, and Adrian, looking taller than she remembered him, coming around from the back of the truck to join her. It is the first time Alice has seen Rebecca since David moved out two years before, and she's filled with the two conflicting desires—one, to stare at Rebecca and, the other, to crouch down against the dashboard of the little Honda. "Let's go," Alice says to Thomas, and he floors it, laughing, very nearly running over the two in the darkness.

Naturally, Thomas wants to know who it is. "My husband's lover," she says. "That was my husband's lover."

"You're still married?" he asks.

"Technically," she says.

"Shit," he says. "You shoulda told me sooner. I coulda run over her for you." And Alice laughs.

But, later, after Thomas drops her at her front door—asking whether he can come in, almost as a joke and Alice saying of course not—she closes the door behind her and wonders if Toby will get a ride home in that truck with Rebecca and Adrian or maybe go back to David's with them after the party, and why he hadn't just gotten a lift with them in the first place. But she knows why, reasoning it through in her head. Surely, they couldn't pick him up at her house. And she wonders why Toby hadn't been more explicit and worries that he might have fretted over the logistics of the party—how to get there and how to get home, knowing Rebecca would be there, knowing his dad was gone and knowing his mother.

The alcohol wearing off, Alice sifts it around in her head feeling a twinge of guilt, feeling the burden on Toby of juggling their arrangements and the tension it creates, feeling for him. So that when he calls at around eleven, she is relieved when he says he's sorry, but he needs for her to pick him up, he doesn't want to spend the night and is that okay.

Alice throws on a pair of jeans and a misshapen old sweater, her hair askew, and gets halfway down the stairs before she realizes that she doesn't have a car, doesn't have any way of picking him up out in the suburbs. She tries to reach him by calling the Bankses' house, searching frantically for the old phone directory from The School and finally calling directory assistance. When, after quite a few tries, someone at the Banks house answers, some teenager, a boy, Alice asks to speak to Toby Fisher. He sets down the phone for what must be a good ten minutes and finally returns and says: "He's not here." Alice is frantic now. She asks who she's speaking to, please, and can he go find Mr. or Mrs. Banks or could she please talk to an adult. Then she waits a good long time before a voice comes on the line. It is Rebecca.

Now what Alice doesn't know, can't know, is that Toby is already waiting for her at the foot of the Bankses' property, at the edge of a dark wood beside the long, circular drive. And that he is shaken and upset. For shortly before he called his mother, he had walked away from the banquet table covered with hearty vegetarian fare and hummus and sweets and the big bowl filled with some infernal harvest punch and started down the basement stairs to what serves as a recreation room of sorts, to get one of Adrian's guitars. And, from the top of those stairs, he has witnessed Stephen Banks and Rebecca Adler, David's Rebecca, wrapped around one another kissing. He stood there aghast for more than an instant and then ran right back up those stairs and called his mother.

After that, without a word to anyone, he exited the building and set himself down at the foot of the drive in the darkness next to the woods, his elbows resting on his bent knees, his head bowed down between them, safe and sound where no one in the world could see him. He didn't look up again for a good hour. That was when a police car arrived. Then a handful of parents from The School came out of the house calling his name. And now they are all standing not far from the foot of the drive watching as Rebecca approaches him.

"No," he insists, as she comes forward and hugs him and says, "We've looked everywhere for you. We are so glad you are safe," and announces that she will take him home now. Agitated, he says, loud enough for everyone to hear, "No. You're not my mother," and pulls away from her. And when she tells him, "Your mother asked me to bring you home," he calls her a liar and runs over to the police officer, his face twitching, all the other parents watching as the drama unfolds, and tells the officer, quietly with great seriousness, that he needs to talk to him privately. Then they both climb into the police car and sit there together for a good long time, while Rebecca and the other parents huddle around the front door, watching and waiting.

Now, when he gets inside the car, Toby spins a bit of a tale, because the last thing he wants to do is get into the truck with Rebecca. For he thinks she may have seen him on the basement stair, and he doesn't want to talk about it, doesn't want to be alone with her. His tic is going a mile a minute, but his brain is working just fine. Thinking like a fox, he tells the officer, "They are having a celebration in that house about the end of the days of light and the coming of the days of darkness. It's creepy and I'm scared of them. And I want my mother." And he says something about his mother being on the Georgetown faculty and her car must have broken down or something, that she was supposed to pick him up and could he please take him to her or call his mother or help him in some way, because this is an emergency.

The policeman asks questions—about Rebecca and the hug and the offer of a ride. And what was he doing here anyway? And how did he get here? And who are these people? And Toby says, "They're friends from school and I thought it was a Halloween party and it's something else and I want to go home."

When the officer goes back to talk to the parents, one of them explains about the Celtic New Year, Samhain, saying it's a celebration and it's perfectly legal, harmless. And when he asks Rebecca about her relationship to Toby, she stumbles a bit with her dark accent endeavoring to explain. "I live with his father. I am as good as his mother," she says. So the officer asks more questions, questions about David and Alice, questions like are they divorced and where is his father and does he live with you or live with his mother. And, finally, Stephen Banks steps in: "It's a complicated family situation. The boy seems a bit troubled. Probably best if he goes home to his mother." Then another parent, an unassuming dumpling of a woman, someone who knows Toby from The School and knows Alice and David and Rebecca, offers to take him home. Everybody agrees that is an acceptable solution, including Toby. Before he leaves, the officer calls Alice, and well past midnight, the dumpling woman delivers Toby to Alice's door.

His arrival causes quite a scene, Toby telling the story to Alice over cookies and milk—how he refused to go home with Rebecca because he hates her and about the police officer and how finally Mrs. Crenshaw had given him a ride, but he leaves out the part about Stephen Banks and Rebecca, the part about the basement, saying only that he hates her and that he's not going to his father's house until she's gone.

CHAPTER 25

Alice & Rebecca & David

For more than a year now, Alice has barely seen David, just in passing Toby from one house to the other or when it was absolutely necessary. She has never once sat down with Rebecca, never seen them together as a couple, open and unashamed, certainly never shared a cup of coffee with them. But now, in the wake of the Samhain debacle, as Toby and Alice have come to call it, Alice has agreed to sit down with the two of them—David and Rebecca, because David is back and has insisted on it.

And now, on an uncharacteristically cold fall afternoon in early November, Alice is on the second floor of the university's Performing Arts Center developing a piece for the winter concert, working with the modern dance troupe, a choreographer, a pianist and a flutist. There are twelve chairs set up in one long row at the center of the rehearsal studio, with thirteen dancers circling around them, clutching at one another, arching their backs, their arms stretching and sweeping and reaching.

Reflected off the mirror-covered walls, the dancers create the effect of dozens and dozens of lithe bodies in motion. Alice has been there for several hours already, and she's enthralled by it.

The music will be spare, written by a student and aptly titled "The Twelve Chairs." She hadn't really known what it was about until today. She had imagined a Russian theme, something that evolved from the famous novel and its various film adaptations. Now she sees that it's based on the idea of musical chairs, the children's game. The thirteenth dancer, of course, is the loser, the one left standing when the music stops. But she's the lead dancer, so she gets the big solo, a dance that suggests sadness and loneliness but then shifts into something more exuberant. "It's about freedom and independence," explains the student composer. "Okay, so you don't get a chair. But who wants to be locked into a chair?" A nice twist, Alice thinks.

She is meeting David and Rebecca for coffee at Dean & DeLuca on M Street in fifteen minutes, and instead of being in her car or halfway across campus, she is in the rehearsal room. Of course, Alice is a punctual soul. She is determined never to be late, as if being late is right up there in the top ten, the big seven, the all-time greatest sins. Envy. Greed. Lust. Lateness. "I'm never going to make it," she says out loud to herself, checking her watch, counting backward from four o'clock. It will take her at least five minutes to get out of the building, and Dean & DeLuca is a good twenty minutes from there, down Thirty-Fifth Street and up M. She's wearing the black heels and the narrow black skirt that she's been living in since fall began. Running isn't going to be an option, she thinks.

The choreographer and the composer are talking the dancers through it. They're mapping it and Alice is there to watch and to listen so she can guide the musicians when the time comes. They have a good six weeks to prepare, but she has only fifteen minutes to get to Dean & DeLuca. "I gotta run," she calls out. The choreographer waves her on. Alice pulls on her gloves, a scarf and a winter jacket and braces herself for the chill.

So she is meeting David and Rebecca, and she is worried about being late. The irony of this is not lost on her. They have committed a famously spectacular sin, a chartbuster, one of the top ten, she reasons. Surely, they can forgive her five or ten minutes. As she makes her way out of the building, she wonders if being unforgiving is itself a sin. She tries to remember all of the sins that are expressed in the Ten Commandments. Adultery. Covetousness. Murder. She transposes them in her head, thinking only of what thou shalt not do. Bear false witness. Worship idols. Take the Lord's name in vain. She misses a few, she knows. Then, she tries to remember the Seven Deadly Sins. She starts with envy and lust. She struggles at little with wrath. Those are the easy ones, she thinks. Then she really has to wrack her brain. Greed, she thinks. All this to suppress the questions that have been tapping at the back of her brain for the past twenty-four hours, like a little man with a sledgehammer: What the hell is going on with Toby? With the three of them? And will they have an answer?

She's left the campus now and is making her way down Thirty-Fifth Street, narrow and charming with its elegant old row houses. She clatters along in her heels, trying to avoid the cracks and crevices of the brick sidewalk. "Pride," she says out loud. The street is quiet, very nearly empty. "How could I have forgotten that one? And where does forgiveness come in?" she thinks. She wonders whether she's forgiven David. "Is it essential?" she asks herself, breathing heavily, gathering her coat around her. It's a question she's struggled with for too long now.

When she reaches the bottom of Thirty-Fifth Street, the atmosphere shifts. She's struck by the wind coming up from the

Potomac and the carnival that is M Street. Kids in tight jeans and Dockers, dressed all in black with lip rings and spiked hair. And crowds of people—working people, shopping people, tourists—all scuttling about. Alice is charged up. But she is determined to be calm, to use Stepford words, to listen and to tell them, at some point, that Toby will not be coming over. For he insists that he doesn't want to go to David's anymore, "not until she's gone," he says. And Alice doesn't believe that's going to happen.

Coffee with the enemy, she thinks. All this time, all this time since David left, Alice had been imagining that someday he would acknowledge her, acknowledge the depth of his betrayal and the pain it had caused her. And then, she thought, he'll feel, well, awful, repentant, bad, sorry. Simple as that. In fact, she hadn't been imagining it—she'd been expecting it. Expecting him to come to his senses, to see things from her perspective. But that's not how it works. Now she believes that happens only in the movies and on television, or when someone enters a twelve-step program and needs to unburden himself of all the guilt associated with his own misdeeds, the hurt he's inflicted on others. It's not about you, he'd said. Now she knows it's never going to happen. The apology. The remorse. The plea for forgiveness. She knows it isn't going to happen today. It isn't going to happen ever. And she thinks that it doesn't matter anymore, that it wouldn't mean anything.

To the left, a few blocks down on the other side of the street, Dean & DeLuca comes into view. It's a freestanding, one-story, windowless brick building that looks like an old train station or urban water works. She's only been there once before—in the spring some years ago, not long after she'd joined the faculty at Georgetown, when they were still very married. They'd sat outside on the long, narrow patio filled with tiny, round black tables. It had been romantic and reminded her of their trip to Italy. She even remembered saying so at the time. She wonders if he remembers any of it. She can't picture the inside of the place, can't imagine where she will find them, what they will say, how they will act. She feels unprepared. She misses the blinking Walk signal at Thirty-Fourth and M, just stands there and doesn't cross, then waits for the next walk signal and steps off the curb. It's rush hour, a jumble of cars and trucks and buses nudging one another, pushing into the intersection, bumpers in the crosswalk. She follows the other walkers, snug in the crowd, protected by their bodies. Once she's across, she has two blocks to go, and her mind is racing. She might as well be making her stage debut or appearing on television. Her heartbeat's up. But she feels as if she's walking in slow-mo, as if her body can't keep pace with what's going on inside her mind. Or vice versa.

When she gets to the door, she stops and checks her watch, lifting her black leather glove to see the face of it like an animated character in *Spy vs. Spy.* She's only five minutes late, for God's sake, she thinks. Then she stands still and watches the second hand. The tick-tick, tick-tick, tick-tick. She goes through this same process before performances—climbing a set of stairs, rushing toward a curtain and stopping at the stage door, watching the second hand, calming herself, getting herself back in sync. It's always about timing, she thinks. She knows that to make it through this little meeting, she's going to have to slow her head down, compose herself. With her gloved hand, she brushes the front of her jacket and then the front of her skirt. She throws her scarf around her neck. She adjusts her mask.

The interior of Dean & DeLuca feels familiar as soon as she walks through the door. High ceilings, cramped aisles, a glass-encased food-service island in the middle filled with gourmet treats. It's very New York, with its whitewashed walls and black details, kind of Italian-espresso-bar-meets-Zabar's. Although it's not crowded, Alice has to maneuver her way down the south aisle to find her way to the tables. She spots David and Rebecca at a distance, sitting at a small table off to one corner. They seem to be arguing. Although Rebecca's back is to Alice, she can see her hands waving about, those wiry fingers flailing in the air. David looks angry. But when he sees Alice, his expression flattens. He calls out her name.

As she approaches, Alice sees that the table is cluttered—a bottle of water, two half-empty coffee cups, and a half-eaten muffin they appear to be sharing, the crumbs scattered about. It's clear that they've been there for a while.

They all three nod awkwardly at one another. Alice insists that she doesn't want anything to drink, doesn't need any more coffee today, thank you. She sits, unwrapping her scarf, struggling a bit to remove her coat and finally coaxing her gloves off, one finger at a time. On the phone, after David returned from Chicago, he'd been angry, talking about the night of the Bankses' party, intimating that Alice was somehow at fault for the entire misadventure, asking what the hell was going on at her house and what the hell was going with Toby. "I go out of town for a few days and my son falls apart," he'd said. She had told him that Toby was refusing to come to his house, that something was wrong, and she'd asked him what it might be. And he grew angry, insisting that she had turned Toby against him, and finally that they get together—the two of them. So it was arranged, except David had called back not long afterward to change the time of the meeting so Rebecca could join them—"because she needs to have a voice in all this," he said.

Now, sitting at the table in Dean & Deluca, he looks drawn and tense, more uncomfortable with himself than Alice remembers. But he begins it. "We're here because we're all concerned about Toby," David says calmly, firmly, giving his words the ring of truth. It's a fatherly voice, a patronizing voice. There's something odd about his manner, but Alice can't quite put her finger on it. It feels as if he's lying, but she can't imagine why he would be lying about such a thing. Maybe he, too, is playacting. Or maybe he's always playacting, which is an idea that's occurred to her many times.

"We all know what happened last weekend. It was very upsetting to Rebecca," he says. "And we're concerned that he get some help."

"I'd like to know a little bit more about what happened," Alice says. Rebecca sits in silence, perched on the edge of her seat as if she's holding in all her energy. But David answers, "Well, it isn't particularly complex. When you failed to pick Toby up at the party, he refused to go with Rebecca. And he was out of control, Alice." With that, Rebecca's out of the gate. She speaks deliberately in her deep, throaty voice and her German accent, directly to Alice as if she is confiding in her. "After I talked with you, we could not find him. We had to call the police to look for him. He was frightened, agitated. His facial tics were very pronounced," she says. "I, too, am concerned about Toby."

"Why do you think he was so upset?" Alice says.

"Please don't misunderstand me. This is not your fault," Rebecca says, without even stopping for a breath between sentences. "But he was sitting at the edge of the forest, waiting all alone a very long time. He was waiting for you, Alice, in the driveway. I am concerned too that he chose to isolate himself from the others in that way. He is not well. I must tell you this. I talked to my friend Stuart, and he is recommending hypnosis. It is a life-changing experience. We want to take Toby to see Stuart and he will begin hypnotherapy. These tics have been with Toby a long time. We believe they are a symptom of stress-related disorder that has latched on to his central nervous system. There is an element of anxiety in it. Anxiety is a disturbing phenomenon. His system is blocked by painful memories. Hypnosis will release the memories and erase the pain."

"Look," David says to Alice. "This could be a good thing for him."

Alice's thoughts are racing. "This isn't about the tics," she says.

But Rebecca interrupts. "There is no benefit in ignoring the symptoms," she says. "This is the underlying problem." And then, turning to David, Rebecca says, "She's in denial," and shakes her head. David drops his hand over Rebecca's and holds it there.

He looks up at Alice. "Why don't you talk to him about it," he says.

Watching her, watching them, Alice feels a great distance from David. This is not her David anymore. This is some other David. Rebecca's David. Somebody else, someone she doesn't love, doesn't even like, has no interest in, shares nothing with. This is someone she is past. Rebecca starts to talk again, but Alice holds up a hand. "Let me give it some thought," she says. "But he doesn't want to come over this weekend. I don't know if he's embarrassed about what happened or angry about something. But I'd like to keep him at home, if that's okay."

Then, before either of them can answer, Alice reaches down, grappling for her purse, trying as gracefully as she possibly can to bend down in her tight skirt and her high heels, her head grazing the edge of the table.

"This is very important for our family," Rebecca says.

With her head half under the table, Alice isn't sure she heard the words correctly. "Your family?" she says to Rebecca, struggling to get up. And as she stands, wobbling on her heels, Alice feels compelled to look away from Rebecca in order to steady herself. She looks instead at David. When she speaks, her voice begins to tremble. "I'll talk to him," she says. "But, if he doesn't want to come over this week, I'm not going to force it."

David reacts, rising to his feet. "You can't keep me from seeing my own son," he says. But Rebecca reaches out, wraps her hand around his, grips it tight in hers and, looking at Alice, says, "Do what you must do as a mother."

CHAPTER 26

There are two twin beds in Toby's attic bedroom. One was Jeremiah's and one has always been Toby's. He is sitting on his unmade bed with his guitar set on his knee. The other bed is littered with guitar magazines, one of them open to images of girls in leopard-print bikinis and tight leather outfits clutching Gibsons and Fenders and Guilds. Alice pushes the magazines aside and lies down on the edge of the bed. Depleted by her visit with David and Rebecca, she had climbed up to the attic as soon as she got home. Now she pulls off her heels, rubs her feet, one after the other, and curls up on the bed.

"I talked to your dad today," she says.

Toby looks up, squinting at her.

"What did you tell him?"

"Just that you were upset and didn't want to come over."

"Did he ask you why?"

"I don't know why, Toby."

"Was he mad?"

"Not at you."

"Did he even care?"

"Of course he cared. But, Toby, your dad and I don't know what's upsetting you. And until we know, we can't really do anything to make it better."

He starts playing again, picking at the guitar. And she gives it a minute. She starts to leaf through a magazine and sees notations that Toby has made on the edges of the pages, indications that he is trying to learn one song or another. She looks at the photographs, the girls in the bikinis. These are not pretty girls by conventional standards. They have long, stringy hair and absurdly skinny legs. Their breasts are unnaturally large, the cleavage exaggerated. They're posed standing up, with their feet set far apart, high up on platform shoes that make them look awkward and silly, guitars in their hands or slung across their bodies. In somebody's world, she thinks, these girls are considered babes, and to a thirteen-year-old boy, this is cheesecake.

"If I don't ever go over there, is that like breaking the rules or something," he says.

"Toby, there are no rules. We don't have a legal agreement or anything. We make the rules as we go along. I decided you don't have to go if you don't want to, and I told your father that I'm not going to force you to."

"Good."

"But there's one condition: You need to tell me what's bothering you, so I understand it a little better. And so I can talk to your father. Or you have to talk to him."

"I can't," he says. And Alice just lies there, looking at him, waiting, until finally he speaks it: "I saw her with Mr. Banks. I saw them together, you know, in the basement. That night at the party." Alice sits very still, digesting it, knowing what it means to her and what it would mean to David, but not at all sure what it means to Toby.

"What exactly did you see?"

"I came down to the basement to get a guitar. They were all over each other. You know, kissing and stuff."

"Oh, God, Toby," she says. "I'm so sorry."

"It's not your fault."

"I mean, I'm just sorry you had to see something like that. I'm sure that was upsetting."

"She's totally warped," he says.

"And that's why you called me? And that's why you hid outside?"

"I wasn't hiding. I was waiting for you."

"I'm sorry about the car thing. That was so stupid."

"I remembered. I remembered before I even saw the police car." He hesitates. "Do I have to tell Dad?"

"No," she says. He looks relieved. "But I may have to."

A minute passes. She is lying down with her cheek resting against her elbow. She closes her eyes. Toby speaks in a great heave of a breath. "I'm sorry I never told you."

"That's okay," she says, thinking she knows what he means, but she doesn't.

"I saw them kissing all the time. And holding hands. And I never told you."

"What are you talking about?"

"Dad and Rebecca. I knew about it, and I never told you."

This had never even occurred to Alice. In all the months that David had been courting Rebecca behind her back—and to use the word "court" is a bit of a stretch—Tobias had been a witness. He had been there, seen it. She knew that. But he was so young, she never imagined that he'd understood it, never imagined he could have told her, never imagined that he'd been holding it in all these years. She felt such deep sadness for him, for what his innocent self had experienced all those many months and how confusing it must have been for him in a way that had never fully struck her before.

"Dad's going to be really pissed off when he finds out."

Alice feels a rush of shame for all that Toby had seen and heard, not just from David or Rebecca, but from Alice herself. Wrath. Pride. "Oh, God, Toby," she says. "You were a little boy. Surely you don't think it was your responsibility to tell me that. Everything would have been just the same. You must know that. It wouldn't have changed anything. It's not your fault, none of it. No one would have expected you to tell me anything. You didn't even know what it meant."

"Well, I know what it means now."

"I am so sorry," she says while he keeps playing. And she says it again. "I am so sorry for what we put you through." And she tells him she loves him, and he says: "I love you too, Mom." And then she lies still on Jeremiah's bed and listens to Toby play the guitar for the longest time. And there in the grayness of the room, she thinks about what she's done and what she should do, and whether she should do anything at all and how to help Toby get past it.

CHAPTER 27

December

Toby has not slept at David's in weeks, has not seen his father, even during Thanksgiving break when they don't get so much as a call—or make one. For a time, Alice does nothing but weigh the matter in her head. She worries at first that David might be angry, insistent that Toby come over, but the weeks pass without any word from him. And she debates with herself whether to tell David what Toby has seen, thinking that he has a right to know, that it could spare him some pain, for she knows now that David had dug himself into a very deep hole of his own. But, no, she thinks, I cannot be the bearer of such news. Then, for a time, she worries that Rebecca saw Toby in that basement and that she might do something to stop Toby from telling. At one point, she imagines that the hypnosis idea might have been the product of Rebecca's twisted mind, a way to erase Toby's memory of it—but that seems too bizarre, even for Rebecca, doesn't add up, doesn't make sense. Then Alice's mind goes in a different direction. Maybe David knows about Stephen

Banks and doesn't care, she thinks. Maybe that is the reckless, unfettered life he wants. Or maybe he doesn't, maybe he and Rebecca are wrangling over it and, hence, his silence. But she has no way of knowing anything about what David is thinking or feeling or anything about their life together.

Finally, after mulling it over a dozen different ways, she decides to put an end to it, to call a lawyer and file for divorce. She tells the lawyer everything, all of it—about Jeremiah and David's leaving and about Rebecca. Alice describes her encounter with Thomas, calling him "the boy next door," and what Toby had and hadn't seen. It all comes pouring out as she sits in an elegant wood-paneled office at Connecticut and K Street, while the lawyer, a woman recommended by Richard Cordrey, nods without judgment or censure and writes it all down on a thick yellow legal pad.

The rehearsals for the winter concert proceed as if nothing has changed in Alice's life. And, as Christmas approaches, she and her sister Catherine take Toby to a concert at the Kennedy Center. Afterward, they go backstage to see an old friend of Alice's who plays first violin and end up riding the elevator to a private party on the top floor, all full of chatter and good cheer. She shares her ritual holiday dinner with Pam and Howard on a night when the boys next door take Toby to a Caps game. And afterward, after she gets home, Lawrence lingers in her kitchen for a time.

She hasn't talked with Lawrence much, not privately anyway, since the night in her kitchen when they had shared the wine and the candlelight and the talk of fireflies. "So, what's going on with you?" Lawrence asks, casual, relaxed. And she hasn't a clue how to answer him. She feels as if she's been living in two parallel universes. She chooses the one that feels the most real, telling him about the new piece she's working on. And how her work is going well for the first time in a long time. She mentions the concert on Sunday and the winter concert and how inspired the dance promises to be. Finally, she says, she's filed for divorce—something she has now told Pam and Howard. "Good," they'd agreed. "It's time," they both said.

Her sister Catherine was pleased, although she'd expressed it in a most unpleasant way. "It's about time you got on with your life," she'd said somewhat harshly. Catherine always played by the rules, and her anger at David seemed to exceed Alice's own—although, at least twice, she'd suggested that Alice take him back. "I don't believe he's offered," Alice had replied the first time, which had been many, many months ago. The second time the conversation went something like this: Alice saying, "I don't think I could ever trust my feelings to him again." And Catherine coming back with "But you have to consider the extenuating circumstances." And when Alice answered, "And those would be?" Catherine had been forced to explain herself, forced to state the obvious. "Those would be Jeremiah, my dear sweet sister. I mean surely you can forgive him under the circumstances." And Alice had said that she hadn't forgiven him because of Jeremiah but that she'd forgiven him despite Jeremiah. Although, even then, Alice wasn't sure that was true. By then she had already made the decision to call an attorney, to settle the matter, to protect Toby and to move them forward.

But Alice didn't tell anyone about Rebecca and Stephen Banks, about what Toby had seen. She didn't tell Pam or Howard or any of her sisters. She knew full well what they would say: "He deserves it." Or "Well, that's some good news." Or she could picture Howard relishing it: "Hoist on his own petard." That would have been his reaction, charming and arcane. She feared that they might start in on her again about getting back with David. And that was the last thing she wanted.

It is very nearly Christmas before David calls Alice. He has not seen Toby in nearly two months. "I want to see my son," he says. By then, she doesn't have to explain anything. The attorneys have done it for her. Whether he'd been surprised by Rebecca's infidelity, she did not know. But it is clear from the papers that Toby cannot visit while Rebecca is there. And when David asks if he can pick Toby up after school and drop him off at Alice's the next day, she asks Toby, and he says it's okay. So she assents to it.

When David and Toby drive up in front of the house that day, she sees them, because she's been pacing and worrying, wondering what might transpire. It looks as if they had some kind of confrontation on the way home. She hears some of it when Toby gets out of the car in front of the house. Doubtless, the whole neighborhood hears it, doors slamming and loud voices and a handful of expletives. Toby yelling, "How could you leave us, after Jeremiah?" And "How can you even be with her?" She sees it all from the front window of her living room—after all the anger, Toby leaning against the car telling his story and David, facing him in the cold, his hands jammed into his jacket pockets, frozen, listening. After that, their voices lowered, they talk for a good long time, both of them with their backs up against the side of the car. Then she sees David turn to Toby, coming closer, and Toby pushing him away again. David must be apologizing, must be asking for his forgiveness, because they are hugging each other. Maybe David is telling Toby how much he loves him. Maybe that's what he's saying. She hopes so.

CHAPTER 28

The End

In February, Alice signs the divorce papers. She has them delivered to David, and he signs them too, without so much as a discussion. It's very nearly five years to the day since David left, and nearly ten years since Jeremiah's death.

Not long afterward, it snows like crazy, big puffs tumbling through the sky. It's a heavy snow that lasts all night and well into the morning, blanching the landscape, coating the bushes and trees with a white powder that transforms the neighborhood, making it pure and still. Everything is closed—the university, Toby's school, city government and all the nearby offices. Alice trudged through the crowded supermarket on her way home from work the preceding afternoon, the aisles crowded with women and children excitedly grabbing up gallons of spring water and milk as if they would all be trapped for weeks or wished they could be trapped for weeks. Alice has been caught up in the excitement herself, and now her house is full of goodies, and she makes a fire and starts cooking up a pot of lentil soup first thing in the morning.

The night before, Toby had watched the ten o'clock news, the cancellations and closings running across the bottom of the television screen like the winning numbers in some grand children's lottery. So he's sleeping in and when he wakes, Alice makes him a big breakfast, eggs and bacon and biscuits and hot chocolate with marshmallows. They watch the snowfall through the kitchen window, then play two games of chess with the deliberateness that only a free day allows. By the time Toby heads off toward the TV room announcing a private screening of an Indiana Jones Film Festival, snowdrifts are forming against the back fence and along the sides of the yard, and the snow itself is beginning to slow. When he disappears, Alice sets herself down at the piano to work on her piece. It's coming together and she is still absorbed in it.

Late in the afternoon, when Thomas comes by with a sled in tow, asking for Toby, she's still immersed in her music, and Toby's well into *The Temple of Doom*. "Where's that boy of yours?" Thomas says, like some woodchopper in some back-country town. She has begun to see him almost as a contemporary of Toby's, which is something of a relief. Thomas is wearing an oversized jester's cap, red and blue and yellow, made of wool and topped with little bells, pulled down over his face, the long, droopy earflaps engulfing his head. He looks comical and cute and boyish. And when he insists that they all three go, she gives in instantly, pulling together mittens and boots and hats for the two of them—herself and Toby—while Thomas goes around back and digs at the foot of the garage door so they can pull out their sleds. Then they walk the six blocks to Deal Hill in silence, hauling their sleds behind them, their feet already near freezing.

By the time they reach the top of the hill, which is crowded with families and kids of all ages and shapes and sizes, the snow has just about stopped, and they are ready to pop. They take a dozen runs, maybe more, the snow on the hill packed tight from all the afternoon traffic. Sometimes Toby and Thomas double up, or head down in tandem, both of them whooping loudly and calling out to each other in a competitive frenzy, declaring one or the other the winner, throwing high fives when they reach the bottom or smacking each other on the back and then racing back up the hill together.

But Alice rides solo. She goes down headfirst at the edge of the crowd with a solitary smoothness and after a while loses track of them and lets herself fly silently through each run, listening to the sound of the blades on the snow and feeling the icy stillness of her body. By the time she's finished, she's elated and exhausted. And when the three of them finally meet up at the bottom of the hill, most of the others have gone, and it's very nearly dark. They walk home, spent and out of breath, their cheeks tingling, their limbs numb. Everything around them is hidden beneath the untouched snow, cloaked in it. Then the moon rises, reflecting off the icy landscape, making the world all around seem faint and glimmery. Even the sky is a hazy white, like a fog. "Sweet," says Thomas. "Yeah," says Tobias.

They walk in single file then through the shimmering darkness, along a path carved in the snow-covered sidewalk by the passing sleds. When they are very nearly home, Toby and Thomas lope ahead. But Alice lingers, watching Toby's figure, lean and gangly, become a gray shadow.

She hears the muffled sound of laughter dissipating in the distance and stands alone unmoving, soaking up the stillness, suspended in it. She thinks of Jeremiah then. Feels his spirit. And, for a moment, holds him there. Then, as she must, she lets him go.

ACKNOWLEDGMENTS

First, I want to thank Abby Rosenthal Johnson—poet, writer, teacher and friend—for reviewing elements of *Alice Adrift* with me quite a few years ago and sharing her thoughts. Abby, your insights have always been invaluable. And, not incidentally, we miss you down here in Memphis!

A handful of talented people helped me on the production side of *Alice Adrift*: Thanks to proofreader/editor Sara Walker for her thoughtful and impeccable work; to Robert Harrison of Seneca Author Services, who designed the interior, for his patience, skill and professionalism; and to everyone involved at ebooklaunch.com for a great cover design and a smooth process. A special thanks to author/consultant Eva Natiello for her continued guidance in the realm of Indie publishing. It has been a pleasure to work with every one of you this past year.

As always, my gratitude goes out to my family and friends. You know who you are—and I trust that all of you know how much I appreciate your love, encouragement, companionship and advice.

FROM THE AUTHOR

Shortly before *Alice Adrift* was published, I asked a friend who had been through some of the experiences that are touched on in *Alice Adrift* to read the manuscript. She held onto it for a few months and when she returned it, she told me she hadn't expected me to get it right, but that I had—that the story rang true. I thanked her for taking the time to read it, which couldn't have been easy. And I thank you as well. *Alice Adrift* deals with tough subjects.

That said, I hope you found it illuminating in some way. If so, I hope you'll share it with your friends and take the time to give it a positive rating on Amazon and/or Goodreads.

For information about my other novels, to connect with me on social media or to get in touch with me via email, please visit my website at www.susanbacon.com